HARD HEART LAND

STORIES

by Jesse VanDeWalker

Novels by Jesse VanDeWalker

Crow Wing

Saint Lucy

To my Grandma Eva

CONTENTS

GERALDINE

One—School Daze, Interrupted

On the gray wall, the clocked ticked endlessly. Geraldine stared out the window and prayed for something to happen. Her world was these gray walls, these fellow students and this droning teacher. Every day she came here and waited until she could leave again. Every day she stared out of the windows into the world beyond, knowing that it was filled with promise and adventure and everything that wasn't *here*.

Her classmates and peers often noticed her, especially the boys, for her taste in clothes. She wore hip-hugger bell bottoms before and after they had come back into vogue and her tops were an assortment of tie-dyed shirts and paisley blouses. She most definitely went without the requisite bra, though her endowments didn't demand much of one anyway. As she sat and stared out of the window on this particular day, she was dressed in the usual hand made bell bottom jeans, with hand stitched patterns in various colors on the legs. Her blouse was deep purple and black paisley pattern, with one of those large elastic necks so that she could wear it conservatively above or liberally below her shoulders. She toyed idly with that band now, pulling it down below the level of her shoulder the left. Out the window, something was happening.

Being stuck in school all day, no one had heard that violent weather was a possibility, but then in this part of the country, and at this time of year that possibility hung over the head of every day. From her vantage point at the window, Geraldine could see a giant black wall of clouds marching across the otherwise perfectly clear sky. Suddenly they stopped, and what had been wall roiled and towered into mountains, into monoliths, impossibly tall and imposing.

Opposite the clouds, the sky was blue and still; but between the two halves of the sky the blue was shifting to green. She stood up absentmindedly and walked closer to the glass, the teacher squawked once and then saw for himself. The incipient storm was miles away, but he began to usher the students out and down to the basement anyway. Geraldine reluctantly tore her eyes from the spectacle in the making, the single new and terrifyingly interesting thing to happen all year, and followed. She excused herself halfway to the basement to use the restroom.

She waited three minutes and then peeked out of the bathroom, satisfying herself that no one was around. The walk to the back doors of the school took only a moment. The big double doors let out on the parking lot, and a great view of the western sky, where the storm was still building. The thunder boomed and the lightning flickered to the left, and the implacable and endless calm continued on the right. Geraldine saw the moment where the storm clouds began encircling the warm front, creeping around it's edges. The wind began to pick up, even though she was miles and miles away from the event. Without warning, the black clouds tumbled completely into the clear half of the sky and after a few moments, the wind died down. Where she was standing, in the hot sun and on the slow-baking blacktop of the parking lot, the temperature was high but in that moment of anticipation she felt a shiver run up and down her spine. Like a tear in reality, with the force of a god's hammer, the funnel formed and began to ravage the countryside.

She was too far away to see details, but here and there the solid objects the tornado was ripping up and tossing away were visible. The sound was another matter. The freight train roar of the thing tore the quiet of the moment before into bloody shreds and ate it raw. Her eyes grew wide, and Geraldine was afraid for the first time. The funnel had stopped actually moving, but seemed to be growing bigger. Which meant it was coming closer.

Her breath caught in her throat as she stared, wide-eyed, at the onrushing tornado. It was still miles away, but the distance could easily close in bare minutes. Geraldine shivered once more, realizing all at once that she was now standing in shadow, the looming black storm clouds had spread over part of the sky where she was standing. She stepped back into the sunshine without thinking about it.

The huge shape of the twister receded, moving away and then took a violent turn to her right hand side and she thought, *My God... I've driven on that road. It's only five minutes away by car. I've seen those houses.* The pieces of debris were more visible now, a twisted metal skeleton that had been an old windmill, innumerable tar paper shingles, barrels, tires, all the oddments of an old farm. She watched the spin of the big funnel begin to slow, and the items it had been carrying dropped to the ground. Slowly it spun itself out and slowly it dissipated back into nothingness, the only proof of its existence the wide and terrible swath of destruction it had wreaked.

The teacher was indignant upon finding Geraldine still not in the basement after the rest of the students came tramping up the stairs. For her part, the girl nearly hummed with excitement. She was going to go out to that road, and see what there was to see, just as soon as school let out.

Two—Get right outta town

The wait was almost unbearable, but when the final bell rang, she was off like a pistol shot, the first out the classroom door, the first out the big double doors leading to the parking lot, and the first in her car. She slung her backpack into the passenger side seat and stuck the key in the ignition, not even slowing to roll down the windows despite the hotbox oven heat inside the car. Quickly checking both ways of the cross street during her rolling stop exit of the parking lot, Geraldine headed for the nearby hilly farm road she had seen the tornado savage earlier in the day. She ducked looks from the other students and people walking the streets until she could get out of town, where she finally rolled down her window. The cool air felt like heaven after the hellish heat trapped inside her car. She turned on the radio and sang along with a song on the oldies station as she hooked a right off the asphalt county road, and onto a graveled back road.

"Pleased to meet you, hope you guess my name,"

"But what's puzzlin' you is the nature of my game,"

She went first down, then up, then down but Geraldine paid scant attention to the road, what interested her was what she had come to see; the ruins left behind after an act of God, nature, fate, whatever had had it's way. The carnage was indeed terrible to behold, and the calm of the afternoon almost surreal in contrast to the scenes of devastation.

Here, a house knocked completely away, as if an ill tempered giant had kicked it apart. There a barn, seemingly whole until she passed by it, revealing half the structure to be simply gone, with barely a trace of wood or shingling or hay or anything to show it was ever there at all. Though she barely noticed the radio getting fainter and fainter, she did notice when the power steering failed, and the car died.

Cursing, she muscled the wheel over and drifted onto the almost non-existent shoulder with the last of her forward momentum. She sat for a moment, not knowing off the top of her head how to proceed. After what seemed like a long time, she grabbed her backpack and got out of the car, slamming the door after her. She bent to check the laces on her sensible hiking boots, which clashed with the rest of her outfit entirely. Foot comfort and support were high items on Geraldine's all time must have list. While she was kneeling, she checked her phone, and of course the battery was dead. It needed replacing; it couldn't hold a full charge more than 6 hours before dying. Instant communication was usually not a high item on the aforementioned list.

She sighed heavily and stuck the useless paperweight back in her pack. She got to her feet and settled the straps of her backpack on her shoulders. Just as she started walking, she heard an engine on the far side of the hill, headed towards town, the same way she was headed.

Three—It Begins

A dusty, beat-up old pick up came rattling over the crest of the hill and Geraldine got off the road. She raised a hand to wave the driver down, but it didn't seem like he was slowing; he roared past her at full speed. When she got a look at the driver, though, she dropped her hand. He was old. Old like you hear about people used to get old, all seamed leathery face and no teeth and worked hard his whole life old.

Furthermore, the arm that was sticking out of the window was... not normal. It ended prematurely after the elbow, looking youthful and cherub pink. The skin was smooth and taut in contrast to all his other sagging and wrinkling skin. The arm had no wrist, but five tiny nubs stuck off the end of the shortened forearm nonetheless. She stared as he tore past, couldn't help herself. His old face had turned just for a moment, moving his jutting lower jaw from profile to face her, and his mouth looked like it had been tucked in by God. The girl was by turns relieved as he didn't stop and then scared and embarrassed as the driver crushed the brakes and skidded to halt some twenty feet past where she was standing.

Geraldine approached the truck with a halting step, not really wanting to get in, but feeling like she had to. She mumbled a thank you and the driver hooked what would have been his thumb on his misshapen hand over his shoulder.

"Put'cher bag in the back." he said.

She nodded mutely and placed her backpack carefully in the box, up next to the cab. She started walking around the back end of the pick-up and had to cover her face with her arms as the truck peeled away from her, spitting gravel everywhere.

"Hey! Freak!" she yelled ineffectually, not knowing what else to say. She thought she could hear the old man cackling wildly, and imagined him giving her the finger with one of the middle-most of those tiny digits. She was by turns mortified at herself, pissed at the crazy old coot, and terribly afraid about her books and things. She stood on the balls of her feet, arms scratched in a dozen places, and dimpled redly in others, and wept with the unfairness of it.

After she had control of herself, she took stock of what she had left: two feet, two legs, and the will to make movement, everything she needed to walk herself to a working phone, or all the way back to town, if it came to that. She started moving down the shoulder, and tried not to gawk at the destruction. It seemed somehow wrong to do it if her car couldn't just whisk her away when she was done looking. Now she was on foot and it felt more real, like it was really someone's life spread over the hills and far away by the terrible wrath of the storm.

She kept her eyes firmly on her toes, and that's how she didn't see the dead man until she almost stepped on him.

Four—Underfoot

He was wearing a police style uniform, but Geraldine knew enough to see he wasn't a policeman. He was lying face down, and his arms and legs were spreadeagled, as if he were a skydiver who had forgotten his parachute. There was very little blood, and what there was of it was mostly around the head. It had already soaked into the sandy bed of the gravel road, leaving a sort of reddish-brown spiky halo around his head.

One of his out flung hands had a brown stick with a leather thong threaded through it, *Baton,* Geraldine's brain came up with helpfully. He didn't have a gun though, and his clothes looked as squared away and neat as if he expected to be on parade. The funny peaked cap she associated with such a uniform; *Guard,* some part of her mind whispered, was tipped back on his skull to cover up whatever damage had made the bloody crown. So completely was her attention focused on the dead guard, that she only noticed the big thing with the tarp over it that was standing not five feet away from him after it had issued a muffled whimper.

She started badly, nearly jumping out of her skin in surprise, thinking at first the noise had come from the obviously dead man. Geraldine came back to herself quickly though, and looked around for the source of the sound. Standing astride the gravel road was what looked like one of those big push carts hotels use to move lots of luggage around at once. The ends resembled inverted football goal posts.

Except hotel luggage carts were constructed of aluminum, made up to look golden, and these were straight, badly welded, unfurnished steel tubing. Except these had a ratty old gray-green tarp thrown over the top bar. Except something under there had made a weak sound. The wind wasn't blowing, but every so often the sides of the tarp would move a bit.

Geraldine stood there, working up her nerve. When she took her first step towards the thing, whatever it was under there jumped and moaned and scared her so badly she had to stifle a scream. Her hand, and the rest of her shaking badly, she reached for an edge of the canvas tarp. The moist, slick way it felt disgusted her, so she gave it a hard downward yank. She meant to jump away immediately, but what she saw riveted her to the very spot she stood.

Stuck through the top bar were six eye bolts, and looped through the open circular ends were leather straps. These straps ended in two cuffs, each lined with soft wool. In each of these semi-benign restraints was a man. They each had different complexions, but it was obvious none had seen the sunshine for a very long time. Their clothing was rotting off their bodies, and numerous scars, slickly healed over burns and fresh wounds could be seen through the rags they wore. Each had an identical ball gag strapped into their mouths, most with a greenish moldy fuzz growing on it.

When she pulled the tarp off the rig, they looked around wildly until they saw her and then the burst into a mad frenzy of gyration. It was that that made her see their feet. Splay toed and black soled, they were feet that hadn't seen shoes in years, or a decade, or ever. They were however, firmly held in place by welded irons. The sounds they were making began to penetrate her shock at their appearance, and the grunts, moans and eye-rolling were, if anything, more abhorrent.

She backed away slowly; and the men who were affixed to the cart began moving so violently she feared they would tip the whole thing over. There was a bad instant when she imagined the cart tipping over on her; being trapped beneath the scrabbling, scabrous flesh of the inmates. The body and the cart were sitting in the low flat between the high hills the road ran along, and for one horrifying moment, Geraldine couldn't remember what side she had come down.

Then she saw the body of the guard and knew, *That way, thank God I have a direction to run away.* It was just before she turned her back on the whole bizarre tableau that she saw a sign hanging down over the sides of the restrained men. Previously pressed between their bodies, it now hung free. Made from an old square of cardboard and hanging from a sturdy length of barbed wire, it was written in a crude hand, in some ochre fluid that probably wasn't ink.

THEY BROUGHT THIS

ON THEMSELVES

She didn't stop running until she passed over the apex of the next hill and then some. Didn't stop in fact, until she could no longer hear the loathsome grunting and moaning and whimpering. When she stopped, she had to put her hands on her knees and take big tearing gasps out of the air to catch up on her oxygen consumption. Even though the men had been firmly restrained, she very badly did not want to faint.

Five—Petunia

"Hello child," said a friendly contralto female voice off to her right. Friendly or not, Geraldine straightened and backpedaled several steps. The owner of the voice was a middle-aged black woman, round in the way happy grandmothers get and wearing a white house dress with green and blue flowers on it. Her face was careworn, with permanent smile lines around her mouth and eyes. The tightly curled hair on the top of her head was going majestically to gray. She was standing next to her mailbox, at the end of her driveway.

At the top of the woman's driveway was a jumble of long timbers behind the still erect facing of a house. Geraldine stared and did not reply.

"You sure did seem to be in an awful hurry. Unless you're one of those jogger types." The woman's face made a little moue of distaste, which made Geraldine cut loose with a single hysterical bark of laughter. She clapped her hands over her mouth and began to sweat heavily.

"Now, now dear. There ain't a need to be scared anymore. I'm Petunia," the woman stuck out her hand, but before Geraldine could peel one hand off her face a high pitched baying bark sounded out from around the side of the house. A small black and tan dog came barreling after his ferocious bark, all lolling tongue and big floppy ears. "and that there's a welcome sight. Where you been, dog?"

It took a few minutes of cooling down after Geraldine had shaken Petunia's hand and gotten acquainted with the dog before she was calm enough to talk about what was on the other side of the hill. The older woman nodded sagely and kept her own counsel with hooded eyes while Geraldine explained. "Well and then I ran over the hill, and here I am." she finished.

"Here you are is right. I wouldn't waste any worry over what's over that hill, Miss Geraldine. That storm was a strange one, and sure enough." The older woman gestured toward the ruined house. "Look at that. Left the front standing, and took the rest. That storm did do some strange, that is true!" Petunia put her hands on her hips and stared deep into Geraldine's face. The girl blushed and looked at her shoes, and felt a lot better, for no discernible reason. Just being around someone like

Petunia tends to have that effect on people. "Now, let's get on down the road a bit and find a telephone." The older woman grabbed Geraldine's arm, not ungently, and turned her down the road. The three of them, Petunia, Geraldine and the dog, began moving across the flat part of the road, and up the next hill.

"Say, uh, Mrs., or, uh, Petunia?" In the way that young people have, she waited for an answer from the other woman.

"Yes, dear?"

"I never asked, what's your dog's name?"

The older woman shrugged. "Don't know. He's not my dog. Came running into the storm cellar when the door got whipped open, flashes of lightning chasing him all the way. I been calling him Sparky, on account of that." Geraldine laughed, and it felt natural and wonderful.

Six—At home on the road

Geraldine was careful now about looking around when she got to the top of the hill, checking out what lay ahead. *Enhanced situational awareness* was what she thought, and for the first time, really understood what that meant. Not that it would have taken much of it to see what was waiting for them. The road was clear on the downhill side, ditto on the uphill side, but right in the center of the flat between hills sat what looked like a completely intact house. The intrepid trio stood and stared for a moment, entranced all three.

Petunia put a hand up, mock dramatic, and stage whispered "Look out around the bottom for crushed witches wearing ruby slippers, now!"

Geraldine chuckled until she looked over at the older woman, whose face was turned back towards the house and serious as a heart attack. The younger woman sobered immediately and took a closer look at the house as they made their way carefully down the gravel road toward it.

The windows were all open, and the glass looked to be in one piece from what could be seen of the front, which was the side that faced them. The door was ajar, almost welcomingly, and the late day sunshine could been seen slanting in from the impossibly unbroken windows. A few shingles had torn loose, and the whole structure seemed to lean a bit drunkenly to the right but that was the extent of the visible damage. Sparky led the way, his sensitive nose snuffling down the right side of the road, half in the grass that grew waist high there and half out, next came Geraldine and a few steps behind her, Petunia, who berated her light house shoes as she walked on the gravel.

"Oooo, ow ow ow! God bless me for a fool! OW! Geraldine now you wait for ah ah ahahahahaooooouch..." Geraldine forced herself not to grin and waited up for the other woman. Sparky never strayed too far ahead, preferring to keep within a few yards of his people. "We've got to check that house, dear. There might be folks hurt in there, and there might be a cellular telephone we could use."

Geraldine replied, "We don't know how damaged the structure is though. It could just be waiting for the slightest push to come down around our ears. You and Sparky should wait outside, and I'll check it out." Petunia took that about as well as Geraldine thought she would, and so they agreed to all go in together.

The door didn't want to move much farther into the house, due to the lean, and it scuffed hard against the floor about six or seven inches past where it had been standing. Geraldine got through easily, but Petunia was forced to sidle in sideways; Sparky wriggled through the older woman's legs and got straight to sniffing. She huffed a bit to hold on to her dignity, and almost ran into Geraldine's back as she went to walk into the house. The girl was frozen stiff, and it was easy to see why.

The interior of the house was untouched. Pictures on the shelves, flowers on the table, grandfather clock tick-toking away in the corner. As if the great storm winds that had picked it up and deposited in the center of the road had never been so much as an errant whistle inside these walls.

Standing just inside the front door there was a pretty little day room with a peach colored divan and off-white carpeting. The stairs rose behind the back of the little couch up to the second floor. To the left was a kitchen/dining room with a big round oak table that fairly glowed with warmth and made the whole room feel like a friendly hug. Beyond the table, double french doors could be seen that would have let out onto a patio, but now let out on a gravel road. Geraldine felt a light bump against her back that told her Petunia was back there, and that she probably hadn't seen, really seen, the inside of the house yet. Geraldine turned around to talk to the other woman, to try to make some sense of it all, but Petunia wasn't there. The door was closed, and Petunia wasn't there. Sparky was though, and he had his head cocked to one side, that universal dog way of asking, "Wha-huh?".

Suddenly, he tipped his head back and began to howl. Long, mournful howls that made the very heart in Geraldine hurt. As badly as she wanted to reach out and console the animal, that was how badly she didn't want to turn back around and see what he was howling at.

Slowly though, she did turn and what she saw and heard was terrible in its wonder.

Strewn about the floor of the house were not only all of the household belongings, that had been so neat and ordered only seconds ago, but also heaps of corpses. Headless bodies, laid down thick enough to put the floor out of sight, and among them was her new friend, Petunia. Her nice dress was torn and bloody, and not so nice anymore and when Geraldine could tear her eyes away from it, she looked up, and floating above Petunia's body was Petunia's head. Light, pure white light poured from her neck where her body should have been, and her eyes were open, and light glowed there too. Then she opened her mouth, and out of her mouth came that same unsullied light; and she began to sing; to sing an old hymn.

That day of wrath, that dreadful day,

When heav'n and earth shall pass away!

What pow'r shall be the sinner's stay?

How shall he meet that dreadful day?

From the singing, glowing head of Petunia, Geraldine's eyes were drawn upward as she saw movement on the stairs above, and floating down the stairs was a line of other glowing, singing heads. They sang the same old hymn, joining in with Sparky's forlorn howls and Petunia's disembodied voice.

When, shriv'ling like a parched scroll,

The flaming heav'ns together roll;

When louder yet, and yet more dread,

Swells the high trump that wakes the dead,

Sparky abruptly stopped howling and ran for the rear doors, the big double french style doors. Geraldine stumbled after him, tripping over the various storm-wracked belongings of whoever had owned this house and the headless bodies that covered the floor. She avoided touching the floating, glowing heads out of pure instinct.

The doors looked out on pure empty sky, with a few clouds floating by. Sparky barked incessantly, he plainly wanted out, and so did Geraldine so she threw open the doors and looked out. They were high in the sky, and had a bird's-eye view of the countryside below. Geraldine dropped to her belly and peered about, and saw that the whole house was perched precariously on top of a tapering spindle of rock, a needle's point that made the whole structure tilt and sway with every breeze and shift of weight inside. Behind her, the dog barked and the choir of heads sang on,

Lord, on that day, that wrathful day,

When man to Judgment wakes from clay,

They were nearing the end of the song, Geraldine could tell, but she didn't know what that meant. Sparky stopped barking and she looked around to see why, and it was because he was running, he was taking a running start and was going to jump out of the house! She quickly stood up, and felt the vertiginous movement of the house as it swayed in sympathy. The floor was slanted downward toward the doors now, and Geraldine had to grab the jamb to keep from falling out.

Be Thou the trembling sinner's Stay,

None of that stopped or even slowed Sparky though, who ran headlong and barreled directly into Geraldine's shins as she tried to reach down and grab him. They both tumbled out of the house, and heard the last verse of the hymn as they did,

Tho' heav'n and earth shall pass away.

The grass was soft and springy after the recent storm, the

rain had done it some good. Geraldine sat up quickly, wondering why she was on the grass and not falling to her death from a house that stood balanced on a pinnacle of stone. She glanced behind her, fully expecting to see the rising jut of hard rock, and instead saw the house she had been in, but it was blown to flinders.

Only the corner posts of the walls still stood of all the timbers and the roof was nowhere to be seen. Something warm and moist rasped against her hand as she sat and stared at the barely recognizable remnant of the house; she jerked her hand away before seeing it was just Sparky.

Sparky, yeah, she thought, *but God, he looks so old!* And he did. There was white all around his muzzle and eyes, and at the base of his ears. He looked seven or even ten years older than when they had entered the house. Geraldine stood up, taking a step towards the house, thinking Petunia but it was clearly hopeless. Nothing was moving, nothing was living in that wrecked house.

After a few minutes, the dog nudged her leg and they turned slowly to walk away.

Seven—Uninhabited

The hill rose to meet them as they walked up out of the flat bottom land. Sparky was moving noticeably slower, but went to snuffle and sniff along the left side of the road all the same. Geraldine was relieved when the top of hill didn't reveal any fresh terror or wonder or anything but more road, and they kept walking. Alongside the gravel was a rusted out old pick-up, overgrown with weeds and obviously useless: they kept walking. Up one hill and down the other and it occurred to Geraldine to ask herself, How many hills have I walked so far? On the right side of the road, a dilapidated old shack came into view, rising up out of the surrounding weeds like a broken gray tooth. She stopped; after a few slow steps so did the dog, and they looked at it.

No power lines connected to the ramshackle building but Geraldine decided it was worth checking out anyway, *There could be someone inside who needs help,* she thought, and carefully did not think, *or who could help me.* She picked her way carefully through the thick brush, there was no path that led to her destination, and as they got closer they got a better look at the shack.

It was built from nondescript gray planking, now bowed and splintery. The nails had square heads and seemed to be made from rust and the memory of what they were supposed to do, which was hold the building together. The roof was a simple forty-five degree angle, to allow rain and snow to slide off, and still had some flyaway bits of tar paper clinging to it here and there. As they came closer, Geraldine began to edge around to the front, where the roof was highest, and she could see the door. It was a simple wood and screen contraption, though the screen was almost totally opaque from rust and fly specks. She could see the vague shapes of furniture inside.

Geraldine pulled the door open and of course the spring made a horrible protesting squeal that sent Sparky up on his tip toes and raised the fur on the back of his neck. There was a table and a single pushed-in chair in the center of the room, as old and splintery and homemade as the rest of the place, and a square hole in the wall she assumed had been a window at one time. No one was inside the small building and the only furniture was the table and chair.

She tried to move the chair and discovered it was nailed to the floor. She looked down and verified the table was too, all with bright, shiny, new, ten-penny nails. Sparky had waited at the door and now began to growl, deep in his chest. As she turned to leave, something on the wall next to the door caught her eye.

It was a simple calendar, the kind a person could get at the bank or from an auto mechanic or the Lion's club, and it was for the current year. She looked closer, and saw it was for the current month. There were neat little red X marks through each day, leading up until today, the day of the storm, which was circled, many times over and so often that the pen had pushed through to the next few pages in spots. It wasn't until then that she noticed Sparky had stopped growling.

Geraldine burst out of the door, scanning the thick brush for the dog, *Shit! I don't see him,* she thought helplessly.

"Sparky, here boy," she called and was rewarded by a single sharp bark, and a resumption of the thick growling the dog had issued earlier. It sounded like it was coming from around the corner, where the single window on the building was. She pushed through the heavy brush, and then suddenly, there wasn't any. The area directly outside the window was blackened and scorched. She stumbled onto the odd patch and immediately a strange cold feeling fell over her. All the hairs on her arms and the back of her neck stood to attention. Sparky started barking again, and Geraldine moved toward the sound though she was unable to peel her eyes off the ground.

It appeared, through the black stubble of the grass, that the very dirt was burnt. Then the smell hit her nose, sharp and unlike anything else in the world, a heavy scent of ozone. She stumbled out of the circle just as the first flash of lightning tore into the earth.

One, then two and finally three blasts of electricity hit the ground just a few feet away from where Geraldine lay, her head covered with her arms and her knees drawn up to her chest. The thunder was a physical force, knocking the wind out of her chest and painfully popping her ears. It took a few moments before her hearing came back enough for her to realize she was crying and screaming. She stopped and pulled herself shakily to her feet using the tall weeds.

"Sp—Spark, Sparky?" she said waveringly. The dog came to her immediately out of the tall weeds, sitting down where she had flattened the grass after falling away from the lightning strike. He looked inquiringly up at her, his head cocked to one side, ears perked up as far as their floppiness would allow. Geraldine went to her knees and hugged him close for a moment.

"Come on boy, we should never have left the road." she said.

Sparky, for his part, wagged his tail and led her back to the gravel.

Eight—The Line

They walked up the hill and back down and on the way up, Geraldine stumbled over something. She looked down, and it was a black oblong shape with a line of silvery metal all around the vertical, with two silver dots on either side. *What?* she thought slowly, not comprehending what she was seeing. She looked to the left and a perfect line of the shapes were sticking up out of the ground, straight into the ditch and weeds.

Geraldine bent double, grasped the shape and pulled before she could think more about what she was doing. It came free easily, making a harsh scraping sound against the rocks of the road. In her hand, she held a twelve inch chef's knife, stainless steel and perilously sharp. She peered closer at it, trying to identify a maker's mark or brand name; struggling against everything to find a hint of normalcy in something, and that's when she noticed the blood.

Worked in deep in the seam between the metal of the knife and the cool, darkly stained wood of the handle the dried red crust was unmistakable. Geraldine looked down at the thin fissure in the roadway she had pulled the blade out of and saw streaks of red in the yellow-brown dirt that probably weren't rust.

Suddenly she felt what could be best described as a heavy thrummmm like touching a huge sub woofer reverberating up her arm from the knife. She dropped it clattering on the rocks and stared at the line of knife handles as they all took up the deep vibration with a tiny, visible movement. Sparky stood at the edge of the grass by the side of road, his hackles raised and obviously growling, but the sound was lost in the chorus of the blades. Geraldine could feel the song through the soles of her shoes now and she very badly wanted to run up the hill and down the next.

Instead, she took a step forward along the line of black wood, towards where it pointed. Her mind gibbered at her, *Run, time to go, vamoose, don't, why, run just run* but her feet and the rest of her body seemed to have other ideas and carried her along to the heavy hum of bloody knives in the road. She reached the edge and even standing right next to the dog, she couldn't hear him growling.

The line of knives stuck in the ground was pointing at a huge chaotic pile of the exact same model of knife only these were coated in blood that was fresh. *It's got to be five feet in diameter* she thought when she could focus on something besides willing her body to take her away from the spot where she stood like a statue. The entire jumble of blades and blood and black wooden handles was moving, vibrating along with the deep hum that was currently shaking Geraldine's fillings loose. Mixed in with it now was another sound: the sharp, sibilant, slithery scraping of sharp metal on metal as the mound of bloody knives shifted. The thrummmmm shifted up an octave and a hump about half the size of the rough circle described by the pile began to move upward, shedding knives to all sides.

Her body's curiosity was apparently satisfied; Geraldine felt her locked knees unfold with an audible pop. She tore her eyes away from whatever was impossibly emerging from beneath the knives, took off in a sprint and almost sprawled face first into the rough gravel of the road as she tripped on one of the handles sticking up out of the ground, again. She caught herself with her hands, skinning her palms and one knee, and feeling the song of the bloody blades ratchet up another octave, strengthening. So much so that when she stood, her body nearly turned and walked back to the source of that siren sound.

She bit the inside of her cheek, adding to the burning pain on her hands and the throb in her knee to keep focus and control. She risked a glance back to see Sparky backing away from the edge of the road towards her before she stood and ran as fast as she was able up the hill.

She crested that hill and skidded down the other side and climbed another before stopping to catch her breath. Sparky's sides were heaving like a bellows beside her as they stopped, and he first sat down and then he laid on his side, his tongue lolling out. Geraldine straightened, arching her back, rolling her shoulders and taking deep, measured breaths.

Just such a breath caught in her throat as she looked across the hilltops at the road ahead. There, one rise away, was the turnoff back to the main road. Her hands found her eyes, actually rubbing at them in disbelief. Before she knew it she running, moving in great, ground-devouring strides. Everything else was forgotten, all that mattered was getting back to the real world where things made sense. Geraldine kept running until she felt something behind her.

Nine—A darkness in the light of day

The world took on the syrupy slowness of a nightmare. Where her running had been moving her along at a gazelle's pace, now she couldn't get any traction, any forward momentum. The presence she felt behind her was growing stronger every moment, and with creaking, muscle straining slowness she started to turn her head.

The sky turned red, and the sun black. The green of the grass changed to the purple of an ugly bruise. In the center of the road stood a six foot tall hole in the world, black like nothing she had ever seen before, a black that hurt to look at, as it hurt to stare into the sun. It moved towards her and as it got closer, she slowed further. The negative hole in reality began to define itself into a shape, the shape of a person, of a man. He wore an impeccably pressed black pinstripe suit, a stylishly pomaded coif and a winning smile. Geraldine couldn't tell what he looked like, but she knew he was devastatingly handsome. *Wow...* she thought, and stopped even trying to run.

She turned, and he began to speak, "It's been a long road for you to come here and meet me, huh kid? Yeah, you've got a lot stronger will than anyone thought; well, anyone but me." His voice was syrup over velvet with undertones of thunder and Geraldine wanted nothing more than to hear what he would say next.

"Yeah, you've come a long way and have got just a bit further to go. The end of your road, you ask?" She hadn't. "Well, that's up to you, Geraldine." The way he said her name pulled things low in her body, and not in an unpleasant way. As he spoke he walked around her, his movements like smoke, like a cat. "Hm? Fresh out of ideas? How about money? Everyone loves money and all you have to do is say yes..."

She saw herself, tasteful jewelry at her throat, her dress the very height of style. She was seated on an actual Ottoman, likely made by a Persian slave hundreds of years ago, and held in her hand a wineglass she knew had been carved from crystal. She watched herself swirl red wine around the bottom of the bell and take a small sip. She sat in a room with a wall made of glass, something she automatically knew was called a solar. The imagery appealed to her sensibilities and private hopes. She watched her other self sit in the solar and watch a man carve a woman as her other self called out special requests.

"Yes, money can buy happiness, and a whole lot of other things. I've come to know you though, and I think you are a woman of simple tastes. A woman who knows that the ultimate pleasure can be found only in the flesh of others. A tingle, a taste, a moment when the line between pleasure and pain is blurred. All you have to do is let me in..." Shivers ran up and down Geraldine's back and she knew what her body wanted, and so he showed her.

There was flesh everywhere, sweating, heaving, undulating and at the pinnacle of it she saw herself. Reveling in the taste, in the smell, in the hedonism, in the humiliation. She saw herself there, liking the feel. There were men and women and everything in between. Items of all shapes, sizes and origins used as instruments of pleasure, and of pain. The squirming forms of animals jumped out at her from the mass; they had been there all along of course. Biting, thrusting, bleeding, hurting, pleasuring and she was at the center of it all even after the only thing she was capable of was screaming *STOP*.

"So maybe the swinger's life isn't for you. To each her own and all that, but surely I've got something that interests you? Something worth ending your journey here and now, with me. You're smart, smarter than anyone you know and before you try to deny it, we both know it's true. I can offer to tell you anything you ever wanted to know, all the mysteries of the universe revealed. All you have to do is come with me..."

Geraldine saw herself in the roadway and saw the man talking to her. She saw herself go to him, and go with him and worship him for all time. More than anything to bow before his feet and soak in the knowledge of a thousand thousand centuries of life. From behind his legs came a sharp, howling bark. Something hit him and gave her a moment, a lifetime, to breathe...

"NO!"

She screamed it, let it rip all the way from the bottom of her soul, she told him no, and her legs found the strength to run. She could feel her will buoyed up and didn't care why it was happening, she only cared that she could use the strength to run, to run, to run.

Ten—Find your own way home

She closed her eyes and opened them again and she was on the main road. The sky was blue, the sun was westering, the birds were chirping and the bugs were buzzing. The grass was a subdued green in the ditch and the limestone gravel a muted yellow as she turned back to look at the road she had left behind.

Sparky, she thought, and he was there. His eyes were glazed and his long floppy ears were matted with blood. Something had hit him, something big and fast and with not an ounce of give in it. She knew then that whatever else she had seen that day, he had been real. She stood and let the tears roll down her cheeks, strangely not sad but instead exuberant. *Brave. Brave and loyal and true.* She turned slowly and began the long walk back to town, knowing she was on her own and feeling both lucky and lonesome at the same time. She brought her hands to her eyes to rub the tears away and it was only then she noticed the dog collar hanging around her wrist.

The name tag was in the worn-down shape of a flower. Petunia, it read.

DRYWALLER

A First

When the teeth poured out of the ripped drywall, his first absurd impulse was to try to put them back in. He dropped his hammer and cupped his hands to do just that before he got control of his body. Slowly, he lowered his hands back to his sides and brought them back to rest on his hips as he watched the last few of the impossible teeth click to the floor. After a minute he leaned up against the wall to peer into the hole his hammer had made, ready to spring backwards at a moment's notice in case of... In case of whatever. His plastic goggles prevented him from getting his forehead in the right position to see down into the dusty darkness. Irritably, he drew them down to hang around his neck and pressed his sweaty head up against the moldering drywall. He grunted noncommittally as he looked at the dancing white dust motes made visible by the afternoon sun slanting in from the windows in the opposite facing wall. He pressed a bit harder with his hands and head and heard a very quiet clicking and ticking that could have been old dry Cheerios, but probably wasn't. He stepped back quickly and mopped at his heavily sweating brow.

"The Hell?" he said while he pretended his hands weren't shaking. He flinched away from a sudden sound above him, but it was just some other guys working upstairs. It was a close run thing, but he didn't call out for them and later he could never say why.

Home

He sat at his kitchen table and stared down at the teeth he had pulled out of the cavity left between sheets of drywall and two by four studs. Back at the house he had pulled off his dew-rag and scooped them in until it was full and still there were more. He had been forced to pull off his t-shirt and tie a knot in it above the sleeves and another at the bottom after he had gotten every last one of them. He sat and stared for two full hours before he remembered to be hungry. Then he looked at his kitchen table full of human teeth and forgot again. After another hour he started to sort them, molars with molars, canines with canines, incisors etc. It took longer for him to finish than he thought it would, and when he was done he sat and stared a while longer.

Handling all the separate teeth forced him to notice that some were noticeably more aged and yellowed than others; some very few had dental work on them, others visible signs of decay. Suddenly, lights flashed by on the street outside and he swept the table clean; pushing its contents into an old ice cream pail. Guilt twisted his gut and he felt nauseous. He only stopped once he had the ice cream pail halfway into the cupboard under the sink. What the Hell was he doing? A better question would be: What the Hell was he going to do?

They were all he could think about while he worked the next three days.

Book Depository

He spent his next day off at the library, looking up everything about teeth he could find. Four hours in, he realized there was no way he was going to be able to learn anything without a picture or x-ray of whomever all those teeth had once worked for. Lunch was fast food and while he sat and chewed he thought about his own teeth, and how attached to them he was, and how he'd probably notice if someone yanked them all out. Back at the library the old maid behind the counter gave him a stink eye indeed when he asked for books about murders where the victims were missing all their teeth. He quickly decided that she wasn't going to be much help, and sat down at one of the computers to try his luck.

The library was closed on Sunday, so he couldn't go down and keep looking. His internet search had provided next to no results. He went to the cupboard under the kitchen sink and grabbed the pail, and then shoved it back and slammed the door when he heard a bunch of kids being rowdy down the block. He checked all the windows and, absurdly, pulled all the shades before getting the teeth out for another look. As he was pouring them out on the table the thought came to him that it was no wonder they had been hidden away in that house... in that house! He physically shook as the idea hit him. Of course! Who had lived in that house?! More importantly, what happened there?

The next day he went back to the library after work. He didn't know the first thing about researching an address so he plugged the thing into Google and spent the next few hours looking at real estate listings and street maps. Finally he knew he'd have to include someone else on his search, and went to seek out the unhelpful librarian. Who he found instead was a good looking green eyed woman with reddish blonde hair. He judged her age to be not more than twenty-five, and her figure to be fantastic. She put away a cardboard box containing some library arcana on a high shelf while he ogled. She turned her head and caught him looking, but only smiled. He was suddenly painfully aware that he hadn't gone home to shower and change after a day on the job.

She asked, "Can I help you?"

He stammered out that he'd like to know about how to get information on an address, how long the building was there, who built it, past owners, renovations, all that type of stuff.

"Certainly. All of that is a matter of public record, but you'll have to go down to City Hall, where they store all of those records." she told him with a serious look on her face. He mumbled a thank you and shuffled away, head spinning a little. He sat down at one of the tables by the newspapers and realized he hadn't thought about the teeth in almost fifteen minutes. Immediately he hunched up his shoulders and cast a guilty look around. City Hall? Who would he have to talk to there? What kind of excuse could he use to get the information he wanted? He knew he had a lot planning to do.

Undercover

He dressed in the best clothes he had, a silk button down off-white shirt and a light brown sport coat with new jeans and black dress shoes. His plan was to appear as a prospective buyer of the place with an interest in history and of course, the renovations. He examined himself in the mirror, slightly smug and satisfied with his disguise.

At City Hall, he wandered for twenty minutes following signs to different areas of the building before giving up and asking someone where he had to go. He hoped his disguise wasn't cracking, the persona he was using would already know where to go. He decided his buyer self was also new in town, which helped calm him down. He went to the correct floor and department and sitting behind the desk was a pregnant woman, her hair pulled back in a severe bun. He'd heard people say that expectant mothers had a certain glow but until that moment, had never seen it in real life. He trusted her almost instantly, there being an undeniable truth to a pregnant woman.

She stared at him expectantly, waiting. "Yes, sir? Is there something you need?"

He asked for the records he was interested in, mentally reviewing his cover story one last time before she asked why he wanted to know all that information so he would be ready. Here it comes, he thought, she's getting ready to ask why...

"That'll be twenty-seven dollars and eighty-seven cents, if you'd like to have a seat I'll go print you out a copy and bring it back."

He closed his mouth with a click, the prospective buyer story stillborn on his tongue. He felt foolish and marched to over to a chair, sitting as directed. The pregnant woman levered herself up out of her chair and disappeared into the back room. He could hear the soft murmur of voices back there and the spooling up of a big laser printer. His whole disguise, his carefully constructed cover story, all for nothing in the face of the simple honest glow of a woman with child. Of course she wouldn't assume anything about why the information was needed, he chastised himself, she doesn't know anything about the teeth. At that moment he realized he hadn't thought about them since he had walked in the department door.

The door to the back room opened and the pregnant woman walked back out. "Here you are sir, will that be cash or check?"

His disguise was still intact enough to know to pay only cash, to make sure his name stayed out of things.

Research, Paranoia and Flirting with Disaster

At home he pored over the pages agonizingly slowly, looking for any clue to what could have happened or who could have put them there. After every paragraph he glanced at the cupboard under the sink, each time a challenge: Tell me what I want to know, before I find out more than you want me to know.

The teeth, for their part, stayed silent.

The documents wove a mundane story: The house was built in 1946 by a man named Schumann, no doubt a WWII GI home from the war and eager to start a family. It was sold in 1967 to a woman named Somers, it passed from her to one of her daughters in 1983 who sold it to what must have been an older couple, as the woman signed her name as Mrs. Fred Anglehurst. A lot of building permits for renovations during the time they owned it, he must have been handy. Then in 1995, sold again to a real estate holding company called the NordWest Group, more building permits, mostly outside stuff like front steps and a deck.

Two years later, in 1997, it sold to a married couple that ended up being foreclosed on when the market crashed in 2009. From that point on, he was familiar with the history: contractors were brought in to replace water damaged drywall and make sure the wiring was up to code. He sat back, sure he was missing something. He could run down each of the names of the owners and see if any sensational news stories about toothless murder victims popped up, sure, but still... He put the papers back in their manila folder and slid them over to one side of the table. Outside, a Schwan's truck rumbled by and he swore he could hear the teeth clicking together in the pail under the sink.

On his next day off, he went to the local newspaper office to start following up on the leads his names had produced. After dealing with a receptionist and ducking the gaze of a security guard, he ended up in the records room with a friendly old lady who seemed to know where every bit of loose paper and microfiche was stored. He spent all day in the musty room, and found not a thing that could have been construed as sensational or otherwise pertaining to the list of names he had.

The old woman came around to check on him every now and again, "Having any luck my boy?"

and "I could help you more if I knew what you were looking for."

and "Here now, I've brought a little snack"

While he was thankful for her help, he was too embarrassed to tell her what he was looking for, besides how would it sound? Hey, I need to find out if there have been any mad dentists or bodies found with all their teeth expertly removed around here in the past 53 years. He thanked her for the cookie and kept looking on his own. He found several photographs that bothered him, though he couldn't say why and had them printed out so he could take them home with him.

He knew he had hit a dead end, but also that he had to keep trying. He went back to the library, intent once more on learning about teeth, hoping he could get a lead from the types of fillings used or something. When he walked through the door, the young woman librarian was there again, her brow furrowed prettily as she stared at a computer screen behind the desk. She looked up as he closed the door, and there was no mistaking the look of recognition in her eyes. He suddenly felt exposed, all his precautions had been for nothing, someone knew. He forced himself to get over it, get out of his own head and get talking.

She responded pleasantly, asking after his last visit, "Did you find what you needed in the records?"

He quickly headed off that particular conversation with a

simple affirmative and rapid topic change. She quirked an eyebrow when he described the toothsome information he was looking for, but hopped right to help him. He followed her progress into the non-fiction shelving with avid interest. She caught him looking when she stopped in front of the books he had asked for. Her only reproach was a sideways smile.

His research was painstakingly slow after that, but he managed to discover that the teeth were subjected to a variety of dental techniques and appliances. Far too many in fact, to have been from the 53 years the house had stood.

He spent the next six months visiting the library, City Hall and the newspaper offices again and again, making sure he covered all his bases. He asked the librarian if she would like to step out with him some time, and she accepted. He got to know the pregnant woman and they talked of the hopes and dreams she held for her unborn child, and he eventually got to meet the baby herself. He exchanged cookie recipes with the lady at the newspaper, and they swapped stories of some of the things they had found while puttering through the old articles in the storeroom. The whole time, he knew he was missing something vital, something that could unravel the entire mystery of those impossible teeth that had poured out of a hole in some drywall.

He bought a set of magnifying glasses and eventually saved up enough to buy a decent, laboratory type microscope. It was then that he made his big breakthrough. The mesial sides of all the number eight central incisors were nearly identical! He checked and re-checked before beginning to examine the occlusal sides of the 4th 2nd premolar where he saw that again the wear pattern was nearly identical across the board. He leaned back from his microscope, sweating and shaking slightly. The only way for that to have happened was if all the teeth were from the same person. In his research, he had discovered that wear patterns on teeth were as distinctive as fingerprints. No two people had exactly the same wear pattern. He shook his head, knowing it was impossible and a knock at the door sent him from shaking to sitting bolt upright in his cheap kitchen chair. He wasn't expecting anyone and he wasn't supposed to see Miss Library until later in the week. Gone were the days of sweeping the teeth all together into an ice cream pail. Spread around him were Ziploc bags sorted and labeled by approximate date. A large, flat plastic tackle box held his various lenses and had compartments for all the bags. There was no way he could put it all away quickly, so he left it all where it was and went to answer the now more insistent knocking. He checked the window in the door, to see a familiar reddish blonde head of hair and a dazzling smile. Numbly, wordlessly, his mind scrambling for excuses to put her off, to get her out of here, he opened the door.

She smiled brightly, "Hi you! I thought I'd drop by and surprise you! Are you surprised?" He allowed that he was, his mind still reeling and trying to think of a reason for her to leave. "Are you going to invite me in or leave me out here for the neighbors to look at?"

He silently stepped aside and let her in, resigned now to whatever came.

She bustled in quickly, saying, "Ah! It's cold! Do you have anything warm to drink?" She was already halfway to the kitchen, to the secret he had kept from the world since he had found them stashed behind an old mildewed sheet of drywall.

He followed without answering her. The floor creaked beneath his feet as he walked to the kitchen.

"Hm? I didn't catch that. You're quiet; aren't you happy to see me? I'll just go look for my..." from the way she stopped in mid sentence, he knew when when found them. Saw them laid out neatly in their Ziploc bags, saw his secret. He heard her sit down in a chair and then he turned the corner into the kitchen.

"I think we better talk," she said.

The Talk & The End

In the end he told her the whole thing. Everything he knew, everything he had learned. When he was done, she sat silently and looked at her lap.

Inexplicably she called out. "You may as well come in here." He heard footsteps coming from the hall outside the kitchen and in through the open arch walked the old lady from the newspaper office. He sat stunned, and only became more so when the mother from City Hall entered from the opposite side, baby daughter in arms.

His mouth gaped and the old lady said, not unkindly, "You'll draw flies, dear." His jawbone clopped shut, and immediately began to sink back downwards. With all three in a room, there was no mistaking the resemblance. Aside from age; they looked, in fact, nearly identical. His mind snapped to the pictures he from the newspaper, he knew now why they bothered him. Each one had this woman in them.

"Sorry," began the maiden.

"We never thought you'd make it this far," continued the mother.

"I told them you were clever." finished the crone.

Once they all had seats around the kitchen table, he listened to their story.

"I really am sorry," the maiden apologized again, "we were just lonely."

The crone snorted, waving a hand at the younger woman while patting his arm and replying, "Mostly she was lonely, and for a great strapping lad like yourself. Not that I haven't enjoyed our time together, dear."

He nodded and looked over at the mother when she spoke.

"Yes, and I as well. We both have," she said as she adjusted the baby girl in her arms.

He opened his mouth to ask a question like who are you people or why me or what in God's name is the deal with these maddening, impossible teeth when the crone spoke again.

"You see, we know all about you, your birth and life and most especially your death. You will die at this table tonight, of acute asphyxiation." She sniffed, turning her nose up. "Choked to death on an insufficiently chewed bit of Hungry Man dinner. A poor way to go, but everyone dies."

"Everyone dies." the other two echoed, and the baby stirred in her swaddling. He began to protest, to tell them no, that's impossible but his gaze snagged on the red preheating indicator light on the stove and the red box sitting out on the counter. The maiden took his hand and gripped it reassuringly, he looked back to her.

"We knew you could keep a secret, and that you were very private, so we rigged up these little guys," she gestured at the teeth and they all, every one, stood up on their roots as if magnetized by her hand.

The crone took a pouch that looked ancient out of her pocket and held it open at one corner of the table. "Come now dears, it's been quite long enough. ᚲᛟᛗᛖ." The teeth began to obediently march towards the open mouth of the sack, and as they did he watched them squirm into new shapes. They were still some white and some aged yellow, some stayed teeth and some did not at all, but he saw red lines carving themselves into each of them, leaving behind delicate black lines that formed squared-off characters. "Runes, dear. The forebear of letters." The crone smiled at him, but he didn't smile back.

The maiden was talking again, "We also knew where you'd go for answers, but you honestly surprised me, going to the library first. I thought sure that'd be your last stop."

The mother winked at him from across the table, and chimed in. "We two knew better of course, but the assuredness of youth cannot be denied but in the face of fact. What she's trying to say is that we want to thank you for letting us know you. We have to be very careful you know, and it's not often we can interact on a personal level with people like you."

The maiden nodded, continuing, "Yes, it isn't like the old days when people believed and didn't have a problem with us. Only someone unique like you makes it possible for us to know men at all." She blushed prettily as she finished talking, realizing her double entendre. The last of the bones jumped into the bag and the oven's preheating bell dinged.

"That's our cue. It's been so nice young man, sharing recipes and chatting with you, but now we must say goodbye, and gods' speed." He started screaming, ranting who are you, who who who! Really though, he just stood up and walked over to the stove, opening the door.

"We've had many names," said the mother as she levered herself carefully out of her chair.

"NORNS," said the maiden.

"Moirae," said the mother.

"Fate." said the crone.

Distantly, he heard the front door open and close. He unwrapped his Hungry Man dinner and put it on the top tray in the oven.

He Knows All the Hymns

It was a Sunday like any other Sunday. I got up after the third or fourth time Dad hollered up the steps.

"Up and at 'em, Boy! Get your ass ready for church!" He didn't seem to mind the mild profanity, even in conjunction with the house of the Lord, and neither did I. I kicked the blankets down to the end of the bed and got my Sunday clothes out of the top dresser drawer. I walked down the hall to the bathroom, where I found the door closed. My stupid sister beat me to the shower. Crap. She always took forever. I leaned against the door with a thump so she'd know I was waiting. The shower wasn't running, which meant she was doing her thirty minute hair ritual.

Dad yelled up the steps again, "BOY!! GET YOUR ASS OUT OF BED!"

I yelled back, petulant, "I AM! DARLA'S NOT EVEN OUT OF THE BATHROOM YET! GOD!" I winced internally at taking the Name in vain and waited to hear Dad's footsteps clumping up the steps to sort out my hash, but he never came up. I heard a soft grunt and he moved back to the kitchen. Darla opened the door and I fell backwards into her legs.

"Out of the way, stupid," she admonished me.

I got out of the way.

The drive to church was always singularly uninteresting except for the mad rush to get our offerings into the little offering envelopes and seal them closed. Sometimes I felt guilty we only put fifty cents into the envelope and then bought a dollar soda at the store, but only sometimes. Dad, of course, didn't attend church. That was for us to do after we'd sat through Sunday school. I was at the age where I was pretty sure I was too old for Sunday school but also pretty sure that what I was pretty sure about didn't really matter a damp little squat. I complained anyway.

The secret of the whole thing was, I was a voracious little learner and really liked Sunday school. I was eager to learn any and everything anyone was willing to teach me. Younger kids have that annoying habit of always asking 'Why? Why? Why?' Well, I was the same way, only I wanted to *know*. Sunday school and church were places where they taught you the big stuff, the heady stuff. How'd we all get here? Where do we go when we die? What's all this God stuff about? There they were, giving us kids straight talk on the hard questions. It was difficult not like learning it all as sound fact. I sat through Sunday school and asked very serious questions.

It was time for the church service, and all of us kids trooped up the stairs and filed down the aisle towards our parents or what have you, except for me and Darla. She always sat right in the front, but I liked to mix it up. Dad would've told me to keep an eye on her, which meant sitting next to her, but if that's what he wanted, he could've come himself. I took a pew in the back that I thought of as the short bus pew, it could only seat two people comfortably and I often had it to myself if I got there first. As it turned out, that wasn't going to be the case on that particular Sunday.

I had just gotten comfortable and was about to shuck off my shoes when an old guy and old lady filed into the short bus pew. I remember thinking, *"Three? Really? Kinda pushing it, old-timers."* I nearly switched seats, but I was afraid they'd think I was being mean to them or something. So we all three squeezed into a pew meant for two: Me, this old guy and what I figured had to be his old wife. I hadn't seen either of them before, which was weird in such a small town. I would've remembered this guy too, he had a really nice cream colored suit and a metallic blue tie with a crisp white shirt on underneath. I had never really seen creases in pants before, but the creases in this old guy's pants looked like they could filet fish.

The old lady was much more frumpy, in a crushed velveteen looking blue dress that was pushed up on one side and down the other so she looked like a cat or a dog that's got its fur rubbed the wrong way on one side so it all sticks up funny. She had some really shiny and obviously fake silver jewelry on; necklace, big gaudy rings, that sort of thing. She was also wearing old lady gloves and old lady perfume. I could tell it was going to be a long day at church.

The old guy sat next to me and he was wearing some spicy cologne I didn't know but it smelled all right. That was good, since we three were really tight for space in the short bus pew. I mean, his leg was right up against mine and our elbows were touching most of the time. It was close quarters in short bus pewville. The pastor started his sermon, thanking us all for coming and being especially thankful for the new faces he saw in the crowd, and hoped he'd see 'em again soon and so forth. I felt like he looked back at us more than a few times, so I looked up at the old guy to get a good look at him. When he had come in, I noted his white hair and eyebrows with just a few black hairs pushing in amongst the white, like brave survivors of a shipwreck on a foreign shore, but hadn't really taken a good look at him.

Normally, when I thought old people, I thought wrinkles, turkey neck, bad breath, balding, watery eyes, white hair and like that; but this guy was different. He had lines on his face, sure, but they weren't really wrinkles. It was like they'd always been there, and just gotten deeper over time. Like a canyon or something. He still had a full head of hair, and if it was thin and white, it looked like it had always been that way. He glanced over and caught me looking up at him. His eyes were blue. Saying it like that doesn't really tell you what I saw. Think of the bluest blue you can think of. No, bluer. Like new gun blue or winter sky blue or old jeans blue. This old guy's eyes were that kind of blue. He dropped a wink on me, raised a leg and let go of a whispery-quiet fart. It didn't smell at all.

Of course I was in turmoil, needing awfully to stand and high five the old guy for ripping one accompanied by a wink but also having to sit right next to him and worry about if maybe the next one wouldn't be so a.) quiet or b.) un-smelly. I took a third route and just tried not to work up a case of the giggles. Meanwhile, the pastor was going on about something something Jesus and explaining that the reading was going to be from the Book of Mark.

I 'm not certain but I'm pretty sure I heard the old guy mutter, "Mark was a fucking pussy," before the old lady swatted him one with her rhinestone encrusted handbag. This was language I'd never thought to hear uttered under the roof of the Lord, and I waited for the old guy to get zapped by lightning or something. No lightning was forthcoming. While this didn't lead me to believe Mark really was a fucking pussy I wasn't about to tempt the almighty by asking about how the old guy had come by his information.

There was a deal of talk from the pastor about baptisms and impure spirits being driven forth and forty days in the wilderness for Jesus and miracle cures for feverish mothers and at each passage it seemed like the old guy had an opinion.

Jesus gets baptized: "Only bath the hippy took that month."

Jesus calls his apostles to be fishers of men: "I'll just bet he did." Accompanied by a poke of his elbow and dirty chuckle.

Jesus cures Simon and John's mother: "Called her lazy and threatened to tell her husband about how the butcher had the same 'fever' more like."

I mean to say, this guy was a riot! The only thing was, the short bus pew was getting a bit too hot for comfort. All the time pressed right up against each other, and it was only getting hotter. I just had to make it to the hymn. When it was hymn time we all got to stand up and sing, which would give me a little breathing room and time to cool off.

The pastor came down to it, finally, "Turn your hymnals to 376: Songs of Praise the Angels Sang."

I stood up and grabbed for a hymnal, likewise did the old lady, but the old guy just stood and clasped his hands in front of him, tapping his tapping his toe to the rhythm. This gave me cause to look at his feet for the first time. He was wearing glossy black alligator boots chased with silver around the seams polished to a high gleam. Not a churchman's choice of shoe. The opening measures were almost over, but I hadn't yet opened my hymnal. I thumbed frantically for the right page, but tried to look cool as I did so. The old guy was obviously one of those stand and hum types who didn't really sing along with the hymns. Not for the last time, I was wrong about him.

The hymn began, and he knew every word.

It seemed when he sang, I could hear thunder rolling and smoke billowing and the whole scene was covered in honey.

When it got to the line about the 'Prince of Peace' I think he said 'Prince of Piss'. I lost my place for a verse and a half.

Every time he said Jesus it sounded like the way I say it when I stubbed my toe.

Before I knew it, it was time to take our seats again. The first hymn was already over and when I sat down next to the old guy, I was hotter than ever. It felt like the heat was baking off him. I sneaked a peek at the old lady, half expecting her caked-on make-up to be melting in rivers off her face, but she seemed cool as a cucumber. She was putting her hymnal back and giving the old guy a massive old lady scowl. I suddenly doubted my assumption that they were married. In fact, I began to doubt if they knew each other at all. I could feel sweat starting at my hairline, both on my brow and on the back of my neck. It ran a cold finger down my back as the pastor began to preach again.

Now Jesus was driving out demons and healing the sick. The pastor seemed stuck on the fact that Jesus wouldn't let the demons speak, seeing as how they knew who he was and would've spilled the beans on the whole Son of God angle. The pastor talked about humility, but the old guy talked about something else altogether, and in altogether louder voice than he had previously.

"He wouldn't let 'em speak, phah!" He nearly spit. On the floor of the church. "I'd bet they didn't have anything to say to the sandal-wearing bearded cult leader! They came for salvation, like any other soul, and he drove 'em right back to pit with nary a word. Jesus," he hissed, "was an even bigger pussy than Mark."

Well, this was out and out blasphemy, even I knew that, and the old lady swatted at him with her bag again. He casually slapped it away in mid-stroke though, and she nearly lost hold of the ugly thing. The people in front of us were starting to take note as well, even though the short bus pew was set back further away than a regular pew. The folks in the choir-nest up above us cleared their throats and stomped a foot or two to let all us plebs below know that our antics were unappreciated. The old guy quieted down. It didn't last long.

It was time for another hymn, and I was sweating like I had just hucked hay bales through the noon hour in mid-August. I stood, and I stood well away from the old guy. He seemed, if anything, more jovial than ever. An odd flush had begun to creep up his neck though, turning his skin from white to a ruddy pink.

"Turn your hymnals to 854: The Advent of Our King." The organ started up and the man's not-so-out-of-character boot started tapping along with it. I didn't even try to sing. I just stood there with my hymnal open to a random page and stared at him. He was louder this time, as if the last hymn was just a warm-up and now was ready to get some serious singing done.

His voice sounded like whiskey poured over the deep, throaty roar of a good bonfire. He drowned out everyone around us and when he sang about the Daughter of Zion, I heard him tell her not despise the piss the Lord brings.

On the line about the Lord coming again, he elbowed the old lady and waggled his eyebrows at her. She looked nonplussed, and it was impossible, but I think his the salt-and-pepper of his brows was decidedly more pepper than when I first saw them.

When he got to the line about the old man being all put away, he gave his crotch a quick double tap and dropped me a wink. I finally looked away and stumbled through the last verse. I took my time putting away my hymnal; I dreaded having to sit back down next to the old guy again. His singing had not helped his flushed skin, and a ring around his collar was turning an alarming shade of red. I wiped my freely sweating hands on my good Sunday pants and tried to look nonchalant as I sat back down. He was pressed closer than ever and if it had been hot before, now it was like climbing into a bed of red hot coals.

The pastor was talking about the leper and how he had such a big mouth, but I had eyes only for the bizarre changes happening with the old guy. He seemed to hum, and by that I mean his whole body was humming without moving at all. His toes were tapping and his fingers were snapping. I thought I couldn't wait for the last hymn just to get some more breathing space, but the old guy could barely contain himself. The pastor was telling how the leper was blabbing to everyone how Jesus had healed him and now Jesus had to steer clear of towns.

The old guy, predictably at this point, chimed in with an unquiet voice, "Probably that's not all the leper was talking about, eh?" He elbowed the old lady again, "Eh?" This time I got the elbow and he waggled full, bushy black eyebrows at me. The red around his collar had spread most of the way up his neck to his ears, like a bad case of hives but without any swelling. The people in front of us turned around to shush him and then turned right back around when the guy grabbed his crotch at them and waggled his tongue. His tongue seemed very long.

He suddenly stood and muttered to himself, "To hell with this, I've got to piss." He marched out of the short bus pew and I caught a glimpse of his shiny shoes. They seemed to have split apart at the toes.

The old lady got up and followed him right out. At that point I didn't know what to think about if they knew each other or not.

In the middle of the pastor explaining the humility of Jesus living in the woods because of his fame, the church bell started to ring.

No one was pulling the rope.

The rope started on fire.

The bell was ringing so hard and so fast the clapper broke off and went flying out into the parking lot, right through the pastor's car windshield. He said later it left scorch marks all over his seat where it landed.

The bell itself was soon to follow, it let loose of its moorings and came crashing down from the steeple into the hall that led up into the choir nest.

The old guy never came back from the bathroom, but I glimpsed the old lady dropping an offering envelope into the box by the door as she left amid the commotion of everything else. It was a strange sort of envelope, all fancy and sealed tight with what I assumed was a wax seal. It wasn't long after that the pastor had a new windshield and the church had a new bell, all without a collection being gotten up.

I never complained about going to church again.

2 AM

2:00 AM 6-16-05

As I write this, I can hear them moaning and scratching at the walls, doors and broken windows. The small tinkling music the shattered glass makes as they drag their unfeeling hands through it scrapes at what's left of my rational mind. Somehow, they know I'm alive in here, and they won't leave. When it began, there were five of us. We were happy then.

"We're young, dumb and full of-"

"Strong Puritanical/American moral fabric." I cut Chuck off before he got started. How he managed to keep Anne and still talk like a sailor, I couldn't figure. It probably had something to do with his 6'4" linebacker's frame and propensity to wear tight T-shirts. She snuggled in closer to him, something I didn't think was possible in the tight confines of the restaurant booth where we all sat. Alex and Jamie, sitting on the other side of Chuck and Anne, leaned against each other, oblivious to our little verbal byplay. They were one of those couples. The waitress hustled up to our table, pad and pen at the ready to take our order.

It's hard to believe it was only three days ago that we all sat in a friendly neighborhood restaurant enjoying a hot meal. I can see their discarded clothes strewn about the living room in the gray light of false dawn. Living room... What a joke.

We spent that night in the heart of the city, walking from bar to bar and then stumbling from bar to bar and then crawling into a taxi to take us back to the hotel. Anne was predictably slobbery-drunk with Chuck while Alex and Jamie were having a spat over a guy that bought Jamie a drink. She had been glued to her phone for the past hour, no doubt faceboxing and chirping about what a jerk her boyfriend was. I remember now, she didn't yell the news. We all thought it was hilarious.

"You guys. My feed has like, all stories about Z-day. Is this some Internet thing that's going on today?" I immediately pulled out my phone and checked my feed. It was all filled with crazy status updates about zombie attacks. I loved it and was a bit upset my internet savvy hadn't clued me into the fun. Even Chuck and Annie stopped their PDA long enough to check it out. We all posted gruesome status updates, laughing about it the whole cab ride home.

We spent the AM and three or four hours of the PM sleeping off the revelry of the night before. The first thing I did when I got up was log in to my facebox account to see if anyone had commented on my detailed Z-day post. I only had two notifications, both from my parents; they had commented and sent me basically the same message: We're scared for you, please contact us, phones are down. *Parents*, I thought, *they really don't get it.* I stuck my phone on the charger and grabbed the shower before the girls could get up. I had to kick Alex out of the bathroom; he had passed out in the tub/shower after we got back. The girls were up by the time I got out of the shower. They were both glued to their phones; the charging cords dangling down away from the handsets, snaking down to the outlet.

Jamie looked up at me, her eyes wide as pie plates, and said, "There's all kinds of pictures up now. Check it out." She handed me her phone, inadvertently pulling Annie's out of her hands as the cables tangled. Annie, who would normally have squawked in dismay, sat in the same position down to her staring eyes and clutching hands with bent, claw-like fingers. I tore my eyes away from Annie with difficulty and looked at the picture Jamie had pulled up. It was a man wearing a suit in full Z-pub crawl regalia and the make-up was beyond good. I could see gore-streaked white teeth through a torn cheek and one of his eyes was pulled out, hanging down against his cheek like a deflated balloon. The suit was high-end as well, possibly Italian; not the normal Goodwill costume suit, bought cheap because it just going to get ruined. I was getting a little freaked out, it was a convincing picture. From the corner of my eye, I saw Jamie elbow Annie and shoot her a sideways grin.

"You guys are supreme assholes!" I said as I flipped her phone back at her.

They broke up into a giggling fit, saying between gasping breaths, "Your face! OMG!"

I turned on the TV and cranked the volume. Chuck whipped a pillow at me from the other bed and I heard Alex groan from the floor next to the girls. I checked the channel guide and tuned into the Salsa Selections channel. "Salsa, fuckers!"

Alex, Jamie and I were ready to get out of the room first, so we wandered down to the hotel restaurant for some greasy hangover food. Chuck and Anne still hadn't made it down to join us by the time we finished, but they had loudly proclaimed that the DO NOT DISTURB sign was going on the door as soon as we vacated. The waiter, bartender and hostess all seemed preoccupied. We left a shitty tip and took off. On our way out of the lobby, we ran into a large group of people that were all standing stock-still in front of the big screen HDTV there.

There were serious reporters wearing serious faces talking about the dead coming back to life. I wasn't sure about the others, but I couldn't reconcile the idea that the joke was real. I was certain it was some kind of War of the Worlds-esque hoax that the mainstream was mistaking for reality. Jamie was already frantically texting her entire contacts list, receiving error messages all over. The cellular networks had completely jammed in the space of a meal.

Alex grabbed my arm; I realized I was swaying on my feet.

"Dude, we have to go get Chuck and Annie out of the room." I nodded numbly, adding mentally, *We have to get the hell out of this city*. I opened my mouth to say as much but my throat was locked. Alex was already dragging Jamie and myself to the elevators, so he never noticed.

Chuck and Annie weren't in the room. We had to wait twenty minutes for an elevator up, which gave me time to recover from what I recognized in retrospect as shock. All the bullshit conversations I was part of, all the laughing over the blue-complected Romero foot-draggers, all the time spent perusing the seminal works of Kirkman and my first reaction was complete shock. I was totally unprepared for the reality of the situation that confronted us. It was Z-Day, we were separated and in the midst of one of the largest cities in the world. I and no one else made the decision to leave the other two behind.

The first place we tried was the train station but Grand Central was a mob scene. I knew it was going to be only matter of time before it turned into slaughterhouse. We tried the bus stations, the car rental places and finally, grabbed a taxi. Two hours in gridlock and we moved three feet. I threw the driver the fare and told Alex and Jamie to get out of the car. We walked out of New York.

On the mainland, things were mostly still normal. We got

on the first bus to anywhere and rode it. We got as far as the first stop for gas, hours away from the city. The passengers filed off the bus, stretching their legs, heading into the convenience store. I had turned my cell phone off to conserve the battery. I knew the possibility for electricity to become unreliable was very real. However, I wanted to check my social network and the sign outside the store said the place had wi-fi. I was in total mobile absorption mode but my app was taking forever to load the inevitable error screen, so I looked up to do the automatic scan-for-women thing that men do when they're bored.

That's when it hit me: Our bus had been the only vehicle moving. There was a hybrid parked at the pump and the store's door was chocked open. The people from our bus were the only people I could see. Not one kid cruising on his ten-speed, not one guy mowing lawn, nothing. I was shoving my phone in my pocket and running to grab Jamie and Alex when I heard the first screams.

In some far-away corner of my mind, I noted that it was almost as if they were guided by some terrible group intelligence. They shambled out from the gas station's attached garage, where the heavy mechanical smells covered their smell. The ones that couldn't move on their own lay still until someone got too close. Others came lumbering out of the neighboring houses' backyards once the screaming started.

I saw Alex and Jamie dart out of the store, him with an armload of food, his big duffel over one shoulder. He was dragging her by the hand; her with an 'O' of surprise on her face that in other circumstances would've been comic, and her other hand held to her throat like an old-timey movie starlet. Even over the terrified screams I could hear an obscenely wet tearing sound from right behind me. I spared a single glance to see an old woman whacking one of the things with her purse while it bit into her leg as if the limb was a giant drumstick. I ran toward Alex and saw his big duffel in Jamie's hands. She was apparently over her shock. We ran down the street, leaving the living as well as the shambling, moaning, hungering dead behind us. We escaped to an unlocked house six blocks away.

The first thing we did was lock the place up tight: doors and windows were bolted. Next, we tossed the place for any usable weapons and that's when we found two of them locked in the basement, shut in the furnace room. We were only able to get a glimpse of them but the image stuck in my mind. One was a woman, her eyes were dry and shriveled and she had a gaping, maggot-infested wound on her right leg that looked like a dog bite but probably wasn't.

The other was a little girl. Her blonde hair matched the woman's in color. When we opened he door, the little girl looked at us with milky, cataract covered eyes. Her only visible wound was a bite on her shoulder. I slammed the door before I could think how likely it was that the size of the bite on the girl's shoulder and the woman's mouth would match. On our way back up the stairs, we didn't look at any of the family photos that might've shown a beaming, blonde little girl with her golden-haired mother.

We did find three guns and a few tools in our search. The guns were a .38 snub from the master bedroom's nightstand, a shotgun with a box of slugs and a .22 caliber target rifle with five boxes of two hundred shells each. I remember thinking: *God bless the USA* and uttering a barking laugh that drew strange looks from Alex and Jamie. There were only twelve bullets for the pistol, but we felt safer than before.

It was six hours before we saw the first one wander down the street. It came from the direction of the bus stop, of course. I consciously didn't attempt to identify if it had been on the bus with us, but it had only one arm and it moved slowly. We stood watching for a moment and then Alex visibly started with realization.

"Guys, the ground floor windows! We have to board them up. NOW!" We all jumped out of the daze we were in and ran to find anything we could use to board up the windows.

Once we had a hammer, a meat tenderizer, nails and enough torn-down doors and busted up tables to close off the windows, I went upstairs with the .22 to keep watch while Alex and Jamie worked. The lone one-armed thing had been joined by a few others and they wandered aimlessly down the street, stumbling over the curb and falling down every few minutes. The sounds of pounding hammers began to echo through the house. It was clear the sounds were echoing in the neighborhood as well, since the few staggering forms in the street first went utterly still then began to shuffle towards our house. I called down the stairs to Jamie and Alex,

"You guys better hurry! Those things can hear us working in here!" As I was yelling, we all heard the unmistakable sound of screeching tires on asphalt. I rushed back over to the window. There was a car screaming around the corner from the direction of the gas station. I couldn't see the driver from where I was but he obviously saw the figures in the street: The car plowed through the things, splattering them across the front of the vehicle and all over the street. One must have been pretty far gone because it practically exploded when the car hit it. The rotted viscera from the thing's gut splashed onto the windshield, completely blocking off the sight of the driver. The car jerked and hopped over a curb before smashing into a tree. I noted for the first time that Alex had been screaming from downstairs since the first sound of the car's tires, wanting to know what was happening. I yelled over my shoulder, "Keep working!"

As I turned back to the window, I saw movement from the car. The driver was still alive! I could hear that Jamie and Alex had quit hammering and were coming up the steps. They froze once they could see what was happening in the street. The driver's side door swung open and a paunchy, black haired man wearing khaki slacks with a white button down shirt and a five o'clock shadow fell out onto the tarmac. All of his clothing was spattered and smeared with blood. He had one hand pressed to the side of his neck as he crawled away from the wreck of the car. He made about ten feet, then pushed himself up into a kneeling position. He slowly took the hand away from his neck but the wound there needed constant pressure.

Blood shot through his fingers in a pulsating jet, wetting the street two feet away with bright red droplets of his life. His eyes went wide and I could see them roll back in his head as he fell backwards, twitching. Jamie screamed, screamed again and was drawing breath for a third scream when I looked at Alex.

He slapped her before she could scream again. Jamie tried to hit him back but he pulled her close and she began to cry into his shoulder. She murmured something about helping the driver. Neither I nor Alex said anything to that. All three of us finished the lower windows.

Three hours later we were exhausted but the work was done. Jamie went to rinse off. Alex and I looked at each other and went back upstairs without speaking. We watched the man in the street. His legs were already twitching and as we watched, his arms began to flail. At first we could only stand and watch. The dead man struggled to his feet. His broken neck refused to support the weight of his head, and his tongue hung grotesquely out of his mouth.

The blood had stopped pumping hours ago, but his whole body was still crusted in red from the crash. Once he was upright, he started stumbling toward the house. After two steps he fell face first onto the asphalt, and, oblivious of the damage he had just done to himself, he started to push himself up again. Behind us, we could hear the shower running.

"Keep her busy." I said to Alex as I shouldered the .22 and headed down to the front door. He walked down the stairs behind me and went to the bathroom without saying a word.

Outside, it was dusk. The street, aside from the crashed car and unmoving bodies, looked like any normal suburban neighborhood. I walked down the front walk, and froze momentarily when the floodlight above the garage snapped on. The motion sensor in the thing had just made my trip out to end the driver's mockery of an existence much more dangerous. None of the other houses had lights on, inside or out. I made a mental note to tell Alex and Jamie that we would have to be on a strict lights out policy. I know now that I needn't have bothered.

I approached the thing that had been a person quickly, wanting to get back to the safety of the house before anyone or anything saw the light, or me moving in it. I stepped in front of him and pressed the end of the long barrel of the rifle against its forehead. The thing's head rolled back from the pressure, and I heard a grinding sound as the shattered bones in its neck moved. I suppressed a gag, and that's when it grabbed the front of my shirt with one reaching hand. I tried to push it away, brushing at the hand.

I was making the mistake people would, assuming that the things were also people and still bound by the unwritten laws that people all agree to. My brushing hand, to me, meant that it should let go of my shirt. To it, my brushing hand simply meant more meat. It tried to grab me with its other hand, but I knocked it away. I realized that he wasn't a he, he wasn't the driver, he was a thing that wanted to eat me. I reversed the gun and bashed the thing away from me, knocking it down. It landed on its back, and its head was caught between its back and the asphalt. It immediately began wriggling and blindly grasping for me, and its head slid out from under its body with a meaty squelch.

I grimaced, aimed the rifle, and did what was needed. The single shot would doubtless alert any more of the things in the area, so I ran back to the house and locked the door behind me. Alex was standing in front of the bathroom doorway, his back to me, and I could see Jamie's face over his shoulder. She said nothing, but stared at my shirt. I looked down at the bloody hand print left by the thing that had been the driver.

"No lights." I said when I looked back up.

I was asleep when I heard it. I took the first watch and the other two took the second half of the night, so the two simultaneous gunshots shocked me out of a deep, exhausted, sleep. Heedless of my own edict against lights, I flipped switches as I ran through the house to Alex and Jamie's room. They were on the bed, entwined in a lover's embrace, with a gun in each other's mouth. I looked away and was sick on the floor. Without looking back to the bed, I moved to the closet and pulled out a folded sheet to drape over them. That second time I looked, I recognized that they had left me with only the shotgun. Crying, I did the grisly work of freeing the other two guns. After pulling the weapons loose, I covered my two friends with the sheet and walked back through the house, leaving the lights on. Cleaning the guns was a mind-numbing task and by the time it was finished, I stopped thinking of using one of them on myself.

Absent any other kind of ambient noise, I could clearly hear the first scratches and thuds as they gathered around the house and looked for a way in. In the circle of illumination cast by the motion sensitive garage light, I could see at least twenty of the things. I went through the house, turning off the lights as I went. The lights had done their job, and now it was time for me to do mine. There was food enough in the house to last a single person for weeks, assuming the power held out, but I wasn't going to stay in the house with my two dead friends. I pulled my phone out of my pocket and checked it. No service. The infrastructure was coming unglued. I dropped the useless brick on the floor and left it there.

6:00 AM 6-15-05

I'm making a run for it. There are enough of the things gathered here now that the rest of the town should be fairly clear. If I can get to a car, I can make it out of this place. There has to be a place where that are more living. If I can get to a car, and I have to believe there is one left in this town, maybe I can find that place. Maybe I can find out what happened to Chuck and Anne. I'm leaving this here in the house in case any other survivor finds this place and wants to know what happened here.

With all my heart for Chuck, Annie, Alex, and Jamie

Marty

SIN OF NATURE

1.

"We can't be sure, but we think you've got about a year to eighteen months of good, healthy life." The doctor was sitting in the chair next to her, knee-to-knee, which she thought was sort of inappropriately intimate until he told her she was dying. Annie raised her left hand and rubbed her temple slowly.

"You're sure? I only came in here for a headache, doctor." She offered up a small smile and the doctor stopped himself from smiling back.

"I'm afraid there can't be any doubt Annie. You've got an inoperable tumor that will prove fatal. I'm so sorry." Annie shook her head, dropped her hand back into her lap and then lowered her head for a moment, her mind wandering to that morning.

Brought low by another one of her headaches, Annie sat in front of her vanity mirror and took stock of her appearance before heading out to the hospital. She was slim, with a figure that would remain tight where it should be for years to come yet. Her hair was straight, black, falling half-way down her back and despite feeling like the bulls were on vacation from Pamplona and taking a run in her head, lustrous. Her eyes were slightly almond shaped, and an unusual shade of bright brown. Her features were currently drawn against the pain, making her high cheekbones standout in relief a bit more than usual and the tip of her straight nose was just a bit red from over attention with Kleenex. Staring into the mirror she dabbed the corner of her mouth to remove some bit of pillow debris and applied some light gloss to her generous lips. People that saw her would call her pretty, but people that knew her would tell you that she was beautiful.

It was something in her spirit, something in the way she was always ready with a helping hand or a smile or a few extra dollars. Finished with her inventory and satisfied with her appearance, Annie stood up and grabbed her purse. She was finally going to see a doctor about the increasingly painful and frequent headaches she had been having.

Two months later and she sat knee-to-knee with Doctor Kelper and tried to make her mind stop spinning after he gave her the dire news.

Finally, she raised her head and smiled again, this time with real emotion behind it. "Does this mean I can get the good drugs Doc?"

He lost his composure for long enough to give a dry chuckle and a nod. "Oh, I think it's safe to say that whatever you're comfortable with taking, we can provide." As he watched her, he could see her eyes dance merrily over him as she leered in mock greed.

"I may take you up on that, Doctor Kelper." Later, after it was all over, Kelper would remember thinking that it had to be a rare woman who could find out her time on Earth had a very real and rapidly approaching limit and could leave the doctor's office with a laugh and a smile on her face.

2.

After what Annie thought of as 'all the necessary noises'

had been made by her friends and family, she got down to the business of deciding what to do with the rest of her life. The more she worked it over in her own mind and the more she talked it out with everyone, from her parents to her acupuncturist, the more certain she was that there was a single long term goal that she had held outside of work and material possessions. Annie had always wanted to start a family, to have children.

Her decision was made when one of her friends said, "But Annie, I mean, not to be insensitive or whatever, but you're going to die aren't you?"

Annie's response had been to pull out a piece of scratch paper and write out the math. If I have twelve to eighteen months, she said, and the average human female gives birth roughly nine months after conception that leaves, hold on; carry the one, and presto! They both had a good laugh, but after seeing the math in black and white she really made her decision. She was going to have a baby.

Luckily for Annie, there were no shortages of 'donors' for her little project but unluckily for that long list, she already had one in mind. After the initial awe and emotion had worn off, and a few awkward meetings, Annie's natural charm broke the process down to a labor of love instead of a science experiment.

Arranging an adoptive couple that would be willing to allow Annie's parents, the child's natural grandparents, to be a part of the upbringing was a little more difficult. When someone was as in love with life and openhearted as Annie is involved, very few barriers erected by people can stand.

Three months into the pregnancy, the sonogram showed something unexpected.

Annie lay with her belly exposed and smeared liberally with the conductive gel and asked the doctor, "Is it me, or does that baby have four legs and three arms?"

The nurse and doctor laughed and agreed that it wasn't just her, there were indeed more than enough limbs for one baby. The only conclusion to draw, Annie assumed, was that there was more than one baby. She found out she was going to have twins, to be doubly blessed in her short time remaining. After calling the prospective adoptive couple, Annie was disappointed to find out that they weren't going to be able to support two children. *Sometimes the math just doesn't work,* Annie thought with a laugh.

Her parents wouldn't be able to support a newborn; Annie had known that from the first. Her life insurance was a dinky little $50,000 number through work, and no company would come within a hundred miles of her now. The only thing to do, she decided, was to throw a benefit and gather enough capital to support both children, regardless of who might enjoy the life experience of accompanying them to adulthood.

3.

In the end, the gala event was held on a lush yacht, large enough to hold all of Annie's friends, family and their friends, family and so on. The boat itself was loaned out from a dealership ("...forgive the pun," Annie often said with a wry smile) that was happy to get the free, and quite excellent, publicity in exchange for next to no work on its part. Little did anyone know, the only publicity from this cruise would be toxic.

The ship set off at four in the afternoon, with much excited cheering and pouring of champagne. Annie was certain after only an hour she and the crew were the only sober people aboard. Annie was seven months pregnant.

4.

"Missing since yesterday is the blue water yacht *Syrene* which set sail from the mouth of the Hudson River at four o'clock pm. It was due back at ten last night, but all radio contact was cut off around seven pm and the last reported sighting of the boat was at six. The cruise, planned as a charity benefit..."

"...NN, your home for breaking news. Still missing is the Syrene, after three solid days of searching, the Coast Guard has been unable to locate the ship, or any trace of her crew or passengers. Experts are saying it is as if the vessel simply disappeared. Aboard are over 200 souls including Annie..."

"Pardon me, folks, but this just in: The *Syrene*, lost for five and a half days has been found off the coast of Massachusetts. Rescue personnel are currently aboard the vessel, thought lost at sea after over five days of no visual or radio contact. Our helicopters are en route as we speak; we hope to bring you pictures of the craft in moments. We are getting word now that the authorities have scheduled a press conference for two hours from now..."

"...Heidegger, head of public relations for the Massachusetts Coast Guard. Let's go to the live feed:

"(Heidegger) Thank you all for your patience. As you know, the blue water pleasure yacht *Syrene*, missing for the past five days, has been found. There is one survivor. Those familiar with the story thus far may recognize Annie..."

"The mystery of the *Syrene* doesn't look to be solved anytime soon, there is simply no physical evidence showing what could have possibly happened. The entire vessel was simply deserted without signs of a struggle, with all lifeboats present and accounted for, and without explanation from this woman (a picture of Annie is shown, she is smiling and laughing, and looks every inch the glowing expectant mother), the sole remaining person aboard the *Syrene* when it was found. Diagnosed with terminal brain cancer and then deciding to have..."

5.

Annie dropped her OB after the *Syrene*. She just didn't see the point anymore. She hired a midwife, a woman who specialized in home births and had been performing them for 50 years, though Annie was her first cancer patient/expectant mother. The midwife often exclaimed over Annie's unhealthy pallor. Annie shrugged it off, along with most of the other advice the midwife gave. As far as Annie was concerned, the woman was there to catch and make sure nobody bled to death.

The benefit had raised over 3 million dollars, after the massive media coverage of the 'ordeal.' She never lied to anyone about what she remembered, which was nothing. Annie quietly made arrangements to change her last name and move somewhere innocuous.

One week after the birth, the midwife stepped in front of a bus. It was ruled accidental.

6.

The first thing it knew was pain. Red, hot pain. Screaming didn't make the pain stop, but it kept on anyway, having no other way to communicate.

The pain became an accustomed companion. Maybe not really enjoyed or liked, but certainly tolerated and known intimately. Soft places where it ate slowly sprouted hard sharp surfaces. These things were accompanied by a sort of slow and steady ache. It hardly noticed.

It was young and scarred and horrible, but she knew she had to keep on. It would have, if given the chance, and Annie knew that.

Hot was only the start of pain, it soon found out.

There were hard things in what it learned was called a mouth, after the phrase, "Open your mouth." was repeated over and over again until it opened where it ate under the pressure of insistent prying. A cold sharp taste filled its mouth and then the scraping began. It was instantly pushed back to that first, agonizing pain and began to scream the old scream.

Annie had always hated the dentist.

Things hadn't been so bad for awhile. There was hitting and cutting, but these were old friends, remembered pains from since before memory. It began to take an interest in its surroundings, exploring as far as the chain would allow. The big one came again and it made a noise at her, exclaiming over the things it had discovered. It knew it had made a mistake when the big one produced a sharp and took hold of its head. After the big one was done it could only see on one side.

It began to crave the light more than anything. Whenever the light came on, the big one came, but still, it craved the light. Finally, it began to make noise when the light came on and off. The big one was sure to notice, but it couldn't stop. One day the big one brought the light close to its face, and it learned that the light was not just light but heat, the big one tied her and left her like that until she couldn't see anything at all.

It liked to draw. In the moments Annie let herself think about it, that's what bothered her most. She knew she had put it outside herself and that it deserved what it got, but there was that in it that made it creative. She took pictures of all the drawings before she blinded it to make it stop. Still, it had liked to draw.

It learned things were worse when you couldn't see what was happening.

It began to hurt on the inside. At first it thought the big one had left something in it, but that wasn't the same pain. That pain was often accompanied by heat, and this was more like crushing pain.

It started having menses. That simple fact frightened Annie badly. What sort of offspring would such a thing produce?

7.

Annie died on a Friday, twelve years after she had withdrawn into her seclusion. The child she gave up for adoption never knew Annie, or her twin sister and all who knew the truth agreed that it should always remain so. The other child, who was never given a name, was brought to the same hospital as Annie's remains. Her examination showed the results of twelve years of nonstop torture. Her teeth had been filed to vicious points. One of her eyes had been gouged out, the lid pared away to leave the socket open. The other eye had been blinded by exposure to high temperatures.

The count of healed cuts and bone breaks could not be finalized due to too much obscuring scar tissue, but the estimate stood at over three thousand cuts and seventeen bone breaks. Her ears had been sliced off, one much earlier than the other, leaving distinctly different lumps of scar tissue on either side of her head. Her genitals showed external and internal scarring, as did her anal cavity. The EMTs that brought her out of the basement where she lived her entire life had to restrain and then sedate her to keep her from harming herself or anyone else.

One of the techs, Donnie Anderson, said later that as bad as everything that had been done to the kid was, the creepy pictures in the basement were what really stuck with him. They were photos of hand drawn anatomy illustrations, marked up with x's and o's like a football playbook.

In later interviews the EMTs were heard to comment that she had appeared as nothing less than some demon raised from hell.

Annie's autopsy showed that she died quickly and painlessly of a brain aneurysm while making coffee. The doctor from her original cancer diagnosis was called in to be questioned rather thoroughly by the authorities. Annie had died without a single cancerous cell in her body. In fact, there wasn't a single trace of cancer anywhere, no inert lumps, no scar tissue, nothing to indicate the fatal prognosis Doctor Kelper had issued her.

Along with all the torture and mutilation that Annie's

unnamed child suffered, the doctors on her case shook their heads sadly when they discovered one last medical fact about her. Every major organ, every bone, every drop of blood from this poor child was riddled with cancer. As nearly as they could tell, it had blossomed everywhere at once, not metastasized from one central area. It was so widespread, they said, it was a wonder the child was alive at all.

DIRT FROM MY FATHER'S GARDEN

When I eat vegetables, I think of dirt from my father's garden. More specifically, the taste of that dirt. It had the consistency of clay, which meant it stuck to root vegetables tenaciously. I was always in too much of hurry to eat some radishes to worry about whether or not every particle of mud had been washed away.

I spent long summer days bent over in what we called a garden and other people would have called fields. We had an acre of tomatoes, and acre of potatoes, two acres of sweet corn, three acres of melons (water melons-regular, yellow and super sweet and musk melons-which most call cantaloupes) and an acre of assorted vegetables. That assorted acre took the most constant care. Tomatoes took the most start-up effort, with the greenhousing, transplanting and crating. Potatoes were my favorite once we got an ancient, rusted, rattletrap machine to drag behind the tractor with the miraculous name of 'The Potato Digger.' Retiring the short-handled potato fork may have been the most joyous moment my young back ever had.

I could go on about my different varieties of potatoes and my aching back, but it's the assorted other vegetables, and the constant care they required, that I want to talk about. Brutally hot summer days in the field, tearing up weeds and filling bushel baskets with produce. We had green beans, snap peas, bell peppers, jalapeno peppers, habanero peppers (those are the really hot ones), radishes (both red and white), broccoli, cauliflower, lettuce (romaine, bib, red, and good old iceberg), cabbage, carrots, rutabaga, kohlrabi, eggplant, zucchini, cucumbers, and for the fall we had squash (buttercup, acorn, spaghetti, and scallop) and pumpkins. Reading that list, I can see why I was mostly in that patch of garden!

I had a nearly constant case of ringworm, which actually isn't a worm at all but a fungus. So I ate dirty food, got infected with fungal disorders, and worked from sunrise to sunset. At the time, the only part I liked was the eating part. Now I can see that those summers built into my psyche an almost fanatical need to work.

While I was doing that summer garden work, my mind was anywhere but on what I was doing. I thought about spaceships and ancient ruins and dragons and rock 'n roll and girls, girls, girls. I thought about stories and adventures and video games and girls, girls, girls. I thought about the money I was earning (not much) and how I would spend it. I thought about dinner and fishing on Sunday and baseball (my hometown team had won the World Series two years previous) and girls, girls, girls. I thought about all of these things as if they were the brass ring, the big jackpot, the reward for my sacrifices. The best reward, however, was still vegetables with a little taste of dirt from my father's garden.

It's been years since I worked in that summer heat, laboring over mud and root and stalk to create a crop. That time was still strong with me when I first met you. I had imagined a thousand different places, things, and stories while I sweated in that garden. The whole time, I never imagined a girl like you. You taught me that women aren't a mystery to solve, a bundle of differences to figure out. You taught me women are a bundle of differences to be appreciated, a mystery to accept. Before you came along, I didn't know and that frustrated me. After we met, I didn't know, and luxuriated in the not knowing. The only thing that changed was my perspective, and that changed my whole world.

You left when I chose work instead of you. We said we loved each other, or at least that I loved you. You wanted me to be someone I didn't grow up to be. I wanted you to accept me as I was. What neither of us understood was that you were really asking me to choose between you, and dirt from my father's garden.

The Burners

1.

Losing your family is hard, but sometimes keeping them is harder. Zachariah knew this. If he didn't, or if he forgot, his mother's spirit was there to remind him.

As a boy, he had taken the family dog to the burners with his father. Even though animals weren't supposed to have spirits, little Zak wanted to give his poor, dead dog all the proper rights before dedicating the body to the flames. In one of the few good memories of his father the boy Zak would carry with him into being Zachariah the man, his father sat up with him all night; helping to prepare the corpse.

They inscribed the proper letters down the backbone to keep out rogue spirits that could possess the flesh, half in the careful script of Zak's father, half in his own childish hand. Next they applied the oils, reduced from a raven's brain, to the eyelids, nose and ears; this was to keep anything otherworldly from using the body's senses to spy into this world. The next step was to seal the mouth with beeswax and inscribe into the soft material the letters that would keep any spirits from speaking with the voice of the dead. Finally, Zak and his father wrapped the dog's body carefully in unsoiled linen, so that the flesh would not be marred, further than it had been through a violent end, by the agents of decay. Zachariah the man remembered his mother holding his baby sister and watching her husband and Zak the boy walk away from the house and down the road to the hearth of the spirits, where the burners performed their duties. The baby was squalling but his mother didn't seem to hear. Her stare bored into her husband's back, though one eye was nearly closed with a huge purple bruise.

The concerns of the moment tore Zachariah away from his memories—his mother and a few of the others were pointing out some fresh sign. He had been on the trail of his sister for weeks now, tracking her through thicket and vale, over hill and river. He had to catch up with her before something bad could happen to her.

2.

Ayelet had been running for as long as she could remember. Running from her family, running from herself, running to anyone who would have her. The life at home, what she allowed herself to remember of it, had been brutal and filled with terror. So she ran. The first time she did it, it was a matter of hours before her father found her hiding in the neighbor's hayloft. She carried her pathetic little bindle, filled with broken dolls and her favorite clothes, to the farthest corner of the world her young mind could comprehend. Ayelet remembered her father standing in the dooryard of the neighbor, laughing with the farmer and his wife. Young Ayelet sat in the grass by the side of the road, next to the post box and hugged her scabby knees. Her father's laughs were reserved for people outside the family. His smiles in the home were a harder thing, all teeth and skinned-back lips. Ayelet was sure that day she would be seeing that smile when her father got her home, and for a good while after.

3.

The trail was cold, and so was the weather. Zachariah kindled a small fire over the protests of his retinue and dug in his bags for something to cook over it. He came up with a jar of green beans and a hunk of jerked beef. His mother had been a prodigious canner of vegetables.

It was one of the few times of the year she seemed to actually enjoy herself, bouncing around the kitchen, full of energy. Zachariah's father never set foot in the kitchen if food was being cooked, the man couldn't stand to see a meal half-prepared. It put him off his feed, he often said, to see the way food was treated before it was heated. His father often said it, and often let one of his tight smiles cross his face if no one laughed. Zak the boy quickly learned how to smile and laugh on command, even as his sense of humor atrophied. His father wasn't stupid, though, and would set verbal traps for the boy. His father would make some comment and the boy would laugh, only to receive a cold stare in return. *Do you think that's funny?* his father asked slowly, holding the boy Zak's eyes. All laughter and smiles dried up. Zak the boy couldn't breathe, let alone form an answer. The situation often deteriorated from there.

Zachariah chewed the jerky while his green beans slowly heated in the jar on a flat rock next to the fire. The meat was dry and tough, but tasty. He looked forward to drinking the sweet water the beans were canned in. He looked forward to finding his sister.

4.

Ayelet was fascinated with the rituals of the burners. Her brother would often tell her the story of when he and their father had prepared the body of her brother's dog and taken it to the burners. In her mind, that version of their father was a completely different man than the one she knew. He was like something from a storybook, something she could never really touch. She knew the touch of the other version of their father. The touch of the real version she knew very well.

After the first time, it was a long time before Ayelet ran again. At least, it was along time for her child's mind. When time is measured in eighths of years—How old are you Ayelet? 6

and 3/8 years old!—a long time is relative. After the second time, it happened so often that the experiences began to run together in her mind. The isolated cabin she found on one mad dash was sometimes populated with a kindly elderly couple by her memory. Sometimes the elderly people were cruel, locking her in the basement until her father could arrive. Kindly or cruel, the old couple always met the same end. Ayelet's memory of that was clear.

Whether she had been in basement or bedroom, she couldn't remember clearly but what she witnessed when her father took her out of that room and into the kitchen was burned indelibly on her mind. The old man was slumped back in a chair at the table. Half of his dinner plate was still there on the table, along with most of his dinner. It was pan-fried pork steak with au gratin potatoes and fresh peas that had rolled all over the table after the plate had been broken.

The other half of the plate was stuck in the old man's neck. The blood coated him, so much so that Ayelet couldn't tell what color shirt he was wearing. She remembered it was blue. There was blood on the floor where the old woman's chair had been knocked over, but not so much that she would have died from it. Ayelet wondered that the scent of the frying pork steaks pervaded and hung in the room; hung heavy enough to mostly cover the coppery, metallic scent of spilled blood. Ayelet wondered, until she saw the wood stove with the old woman shoved into it headfirst. Ayelet knew better than to scream. He father laid a heavy hand on her shoulder from behind her. Ayelet knew better than to scream.

"They knew this was your fault, Aya."

She hated the pet name her father had given her. In that moment, Ayelet realized it was more than just the name she hated: She hated her father. In that moment, she hated him more than she feared him.

"They won't get any of the proper rites. No letters, no oils, no Burners to pray them safely away. These two will stick with me. They knew it was your fault, so the next time you run? They'll help me find you."

Ayelet's moment of terrible, powerful hatred passed and she feared her father more than ever. It still wasn't long before she ran again.

5.

The morning brought back the sun and warmer weather. Zachariah took it as a good portent and started in the direction of the nearest settlement. Ayelet was no hunter of wild game, and at some point she would need to eat. His mother had always chided his sister's eating, saying she pecked like a bird, hardly eating anything at all. As he walked toward town, Zachariah remembered the last meal his mother ever cooked for the family.

The table was set: knives on the left; forks on the right; glasses set to the upper left of the plates; napkins trifolded and set in the center of the plates; chairs pushed in against the table. Zak the boy had been setting the table for years. It had been difficult to learn the exact placement of all the items but his father noted every small mistake. Zak and his mother had once gone a week without food while the boy learned to trifold the napkins correctly each time. If a single item was out of place at table, his father could eat but Zak the boy, his mother and eventually his sister would have to sit and stare at their empty plates. His father always took the leftover food and used it to slop the hogs. It was a hard lesson to learn, but Zachariah the man knew that in many things in life; there is only one chance. Perfection was the goal.

The last meal the family shared together was a beef roast that his mother simmered all day with carrots, potatoes, onions, rutabaga and mushrooms. The whole house smelled of the savory juices of the slow-cooking meat. Zak the boy's mouth watered at the thought of the beef that would practically melt in his mouth. His mind was so wrapped up in the reverie that he didn't notice when he put down his sister's knife with the edge facing inwards, toward the plate. Zak the boy didn't notice, but his father did. The man sat at the table, mopping up the brown juices of the roast with a piece of bread while the family sat with empty plates. Ayelet, who was too young to know better, stared at every move her father's hands made. Her little tummy made near-constant growls, complaining of its emptiness. Zak the boy stared at his empty plate, the trifold napkin folded and positioned perfectly, the utensils placed correctly and cursed himself for an idiot. Roast beef was his absolute favorite. His father stood up, rubbing his stomach and belching a contented belch.

The roast would have been enough food for two or three meals and Zak's mother always used the leftovers to make beef stew; another of the boy's favorites. His father moved to the pot, putting on the heavy mitts in preparation of handling the hot kettle to carry the meal out to the hogs.

"no"

At first, Zak thought it was a voice in his own mind. After all, he had been screaming the word in his head since the discovery of the mislaid knife. It wasn't a voice in his mind, though. The tiny little word came from the end of the table, where his sister sat. His father stopped moving, still as a statue, unsure himself of what he had heard. Ayelet, mistaking their father's body language entirely, said it again with more conviction.

"No. I hungry, Daddy."

In the short history of Zak the boy's life, never had such a thing occurred. His father said 'no' to him, to his mother, to anyone at all. No one else was allowed that word. Not in that house. Not to that man. Zak the boy watched his father carefully. The roast still steamed in the pot. His father's teeth began to show as the lips were skinned back. Blind people might have described it as a smile. His father moved toward Ayelet, hefting the pot over her head.

"No? You hungry, Aya? Open your mouth, then." his father said.

Zak the boy knew what was next, and so did his mother. Her chair shot back and tipped over with the force of her jumping to her feet.

"NO! You will not! She's just a child! If you..."

"I won't." his father said under his breath as he swung the kettle away from Ayelet.

Zak the boy spent the next several days changing the bandages on his mother's scalded face, hands and arms. She went from bad to worse until finally, she shivered and shook and died laying in Zak's bed. His father watched as Zak dug the grave.

The next morning, the grave was empty and Zak found the dress he had picked out for his mother in the hog pen.

6.

Ayelet stumbled through the little hamlet, afraid and hungry. She hadn't eaten in three days but she knew that anyone who helped her was doomed. Her father had taught her that lesson very well. The old couple, a traveling merchant and his wagon, a tattoo artist, a poetic hermit and her own mother. All dead, for the crime of helping Ayelet. It didn't stop her from running, but she had stopped looking for help. The little town was made of four houses and a spirit hearth, where the Burners did their work for the next world. Ayelet was hungry and afraid.

7.

Zak the boy bided his time. He watched Aya run, over and over. He kept the home place each time until their father brought her back. Zak the boy became Zachariah the man. On the day he reached seventeen winters, Aya ran again. Zak the boy watched his father prepare the tracking kit: the bundle of incense to burn when the trail went cold; the cat's eye ointment for spotting the tracks; and so on. Zak the boy had seen the process enough times to know what went in the pack and how it was used. Since the day of her exhumation and consequent dumping of her body to slop the hogs, Zak had listened to his mother explain how to use all of the arcane items. His father shouldered the pack and turned back to Zak before walking out of the house, and his father had that baring of teeth the man used as a smile on his lips.

"I'll bring her back. For the both of us." His father stepped out onto the stoop, adjusting his pack one last time before walking down the road to track, find and bring back Aya. Zak picked up the big rock the family used to hold the front door open in the summer. Zak the boy lifted it over his head and smashed it down on the back of his father's neck. Zachariah the man stood over the fallen form of his father. He watched the breath still come into his father's body. Zachariah knew his father carried the spirits of all those people that had helped Aya run away with him. If his father died, Zachariah knew those spirits would cling to his own living body, like the uncleansed spirit of his mother had. Zachariah also knew that if he didn't give the corpse of his father all the rites and the flame, his father's spirit too would linger on. He stripped the pack off of the paralyzed, breathing vegetable in the dooryard. Zachariah had to find his sister before something bad could happen.

8.

Ayelet never had many things to call her own. What little she did have, she squirreled away over years of careful hoarding and planning. Her father always horrifically murdered anyone who gave her shelter or a helping hand but he never asked why she sought out the people she ran to. From the poet she learned all the letters; from the merchant she got and hid all the materials; the tattoo artist didn't want to give her the letters on her back but her father taught her how to persuade men, inadvertently; the old man was a pewtersmith, and she got type casts of the letters. Ayelet had run her whole life, but now she was running to something rather than away. The burners, priests who watched over those who would burn and ushered their spirits on to the next life, exclaimed at her piety when they saw the tattoos of the holy letters down her backbone. They marveled at her dedication in applying her own beeswax and oils. Solemnly, they wrapped her in the unsoiled linens. They were just finished when the doors to the hearth of the spirits burst open.

9.

Zachariah the man had found his sister, Aya, so now something bad could happen.

10.

She listened to the priests dying, knowing her father was killing them. The sounds were muffled through the linen. She couldn't see it, but Ayelet could feel the heat from the flames burning in the hearth of the spirits. As best she was able, Ayelet ran towards freedom.

BIG WORK

He thought about what he had done to get the order for the family Follic. He didn't like where that was headed so he stopped and looked at the sky. There, the clouds moved and formed his Dad's face.

"Son, you'll never get away from the law like that. You have to get some kinda transportation! Stay ahead of their radio net!"

He nodded, resigned. His Dad never had much to say about current events, but he was an excellent source of info about avoiding police, whatever they were.

The world was empty. Mostly empty, anyway. There were still people here and there, like himself and the Follicses. Those people sometimes needed things that were hard to get, and that's how he got by. His name was Ells. His real name had the initials L.L.L., and his Dad called him 'Ells'. That was how he introduced himself to other people, when he met them.

"Who are you? What do you want with us?" people would ask, usually scared.

"Me? I'm Ells, and it's not about what I want, it's about what I can get you." he'd say, with his best smile.

Even though most of the people had gone, the world was

not uninhabited. Vegetables and grain could still be grown, and there was plenty of sunshine and rain and winter and summer to go around. A few lucky ones here and there had managed to keep some chickens or other livestock alive. It was the oil bug that had done for the world, mostly. A tiny little bugger that was made to eat up oil slicks on the ocean. Turned out it was still hungry after the oil slicks were all gone. Soon after the oil was gone, mostly the people were, too.

Ells walked down the smooth tarmac, the zippers on his leather vest making a soft jingling music. He put one foot in front of the other, over and over, and that was how he got new places. Most people that were left were too scared to travel anywhere, and rightfully so. Even though there weren't so many people, there were other live things. Things that got the little oil bug in them and then changed. He had always wanted to travel though, and see what there was to see over the next hill, and past the next river and on the other side of those woods. It was a lonely life, and a scary one, but he did it all safe in the knowledge he would never be caught by the U.S. Marshals or the FBI or any of those types. His Dad knew all about how to get away from them.

The countryside here was mostly the long grasses and flat land that had once been an ocean of prairie. He looked around and watched the grass move like waves when the wind blew, and watched the grass bake and shimmer in the high heat of the day and he put one foot in front of the other and moved towards the Follic home. Many people that were left liked to live in high places or flat places so they could see trouble coming from a long ways off. Ells never saw the point of that, trouble was going to come to you whether you saw it coming or not. Better to just be ready for trouble, than worrying over if you could see it or not, was how his Dad had raised him up to be. He didn't really remember a time that wasn't this time, not really.

His pack on his back had white stains on the edges of all

the straps that looked a bit like wood grain. He had worn it so long and hard that the ages of sweat could be counted by the rings. It had never rotted or fallen apart yet, and he liked the earthy smell of it. It was windy now, and the grasses moved prettily. He watched them carefully. That was part of being ready for trouble, the watching. Even though his Dad wasn't up on all the news that was fit to print, he still sometimes told Ells to look out for that stand of trees or that stagnant pond or those grasses right there that are only bending from their midpoint when the wind blows.

Ells stopped and stared at the spot where the grasses had moved differently. He slowly shifted his pack and set it carefully on the ground, never moving his eyes off the spot. His hand settled on the straps that held his machete in place while he walked and began unsnapping them. The noise they made seemed loud even though the wind was blowing and the bugs were buzzing.

He drew out his machete, which when he had asked his Dad what machete meant the man had said, "Big work knife," and been pretty well right on. He stood and waited and stared and watched for the thing in the grass to make its move.

When it came, it came fast. Its long limbs whipped out of the grass, tipped with bunches of hooked claws and Ells rolled aside as they slapped down on the pavement with oddly normal-sounding meaty thuds. He sheared through one before the thing could pull it back for another go. The flesh was the dull orange of very old road safety cones but the blood was startlingly red on the sun-washed road. Blood was still blood, anyway. It reared up out of the grass, and it was a Roadish.

The Roadish has an amorphous body, from which depend an always odd number—3,5,7,9—of long, hose-like appendages. It is with these that it performs a really disturbing form of locomotion. Rising up out of the morass of its body is a head that sort of looks like a horse's head but with two basketball sized blaze orange eyes and some number of purple nodules that look like normal eyes, but are scattered hither and yon about the head. It uses the eyes to see and the nodules to echolocate and that's how it hunts. It lays there with its head pressed to the ground, hearing prey putting one foot in front of the other until the food is close enough to grab and eat. Ells didn't know where it puts the food, the Roadish having no visible mouth of any kind, and he wasn't in any hurry to find out.

He stood ready on the road, machete held loosely in one hand while the other was held out from his body, fingers splayed apart, feeling the wind blow. He didn't look at any one part of the Roadish, but watched the whole thing for general movement. It made a weird trilling sound, and turned its big compound bug eyes at him. It sort of shuddered and the hooked claws came flying at him again and this time he stood his ground. It sent three at him, so he knew it had at least one in reserve, due to him having already cut one. He leaned out of the way as one missed him on the right, and then he stomped down hard on it, his big, blocky boots making crunching and squishing sounds and the claws at the end of the thing clicked busily against the pavement. One was headed right for his face, so he ducked it and made a half moon shaped arc with the machete, knocking the limb away and slicing into it. He tried to grab the third one to keep it from grabbing him, and the thick bristly hairs poking up out of the mottled orange flesh revolted him. He made a bad job of it though, and it grabbed him instead.

Now is when the Roadish brought out its odd numbered last limb and wrapped it around his right leg. The arm with the machete was still free, and it hadn't yet pulled him off balance and exactly that much was right in the world. He sliced through the limb wrapped around his left arm where it had started to get taut. The sliced end was dragged back, but the remains held tight to his arm, claws digging into him through his shirt. Then his leg was yanked out from under him and he fell down. The Roadish pulled him toward itself, and Ells found out where the thing kept its mouth.

The entirety of the Roadish's head split open crossways, revealing a jaw with four hinges and rows of teeth. At the center was a big black hole where, Ells supposed, it meant for him to go. He glanced up for just a second, but the clouds didn't move or anything, so he got back to the work at hand. He was at the edge of the road now, being dragged not exactly quickly towards the lowered, split-apart head of the Roadish. His machete had a strap on it to keep him from dropping it, and it had done its job. He got a grip on the handle and got ready to do some big work.

The adrenaline helped of course, but it was probably the best sit-up he had ever done. He bent double and hacked through the line of limb that connected him to the thing. The head snapped open and closed, inches from his boot. He scuttled awkwardly backwards away from it. He stood up, peeled the still clutching limbs and claws off of him and looked at it. He could have left it there, crippled and hungry, but one of the other things he didn't know about the Roadish was how fast it healed.

The cuts had been fairly deep where the hooked claws had gouged him, so he washed them out with his emergency whiskey after taking an emergency pull to stem the pain and settle his nerves. He was bleeding a fair amount from the damage he had taken and knew he had to get that stopped right away. He hated taking a hit high on an arm. It made bandaging a real bitch. He glanced over at the dead Roadish, wondering what kind of things would come to eat it, now that it was dead. As he worked he looked up now and again, and saw that his Dad was back, but not saying anything. Just watching and frowning in concentration. He did that, sometimes.

It had been a long walk, a lot of putting one foot in front of the other, to get here. Here was a little valley, a place where there was only one main road that went through. Someone a long time ago had decided it would make a good place for a town, and so there was what once would have been a pretty little ville. A river ran through the place, offering fresh water and waste disposal and he supposed that was why the Follicses lived there. He stood at one end of the place and could see the sky at the other end, but it was a clear blue, not a cloud in sight. That was a good thing, since Dad was full of cautionary tales about the dangers of small towns to the man on the run.

The duraluminum siding on the houses and buildings looked as good as the day it had been installed, but most of the windows were broken and the doors hung oddly from the frames' warping. The yards were all run to riot, with here and there a tree pushing up through a house. Various humps could be seen in the long vegetation of the yards, reminding Ells uncomfortably of the Roadish. He stayed right in the middle of the street. The way you could tell that a bunch of people had lived here was, all the cars were gone. The bug had taken a long time to get to the cars, and they were gold mines of salvage. He walked down the middle of the cleared street towards the Follic home and didn't look at anything in particular. The thought came to him that even though there was only two easy ways in or out of the valley, neither was watched or guarded against trouble. That bothered him, and he didn't know why.

The Follic's house had a real yard, mowed with precision. The house was pristine and well cared for. The image of it stuck in his mind like a popcorn hull sticks in the roof of a person's mouth. He kept working at it, trying to think his way around it, trying to figure out not how but *why*?

He gave up and concentrated on putting one foot in front of the other to get up their driveway. The house was white with fake black shutters nailed on outside the windows. It sat on the corner of its block, near to the street on two sides with a neighbor only on what was the back side of the house, and on the other side was a big empty field. A two car garage sat on the left and further away on the field side was another small outbuilding with a garage door. As he moved forward, he could see the side door that faced the garage; this was the main door they used, instead of the door on the front of the house. It was open except for the outer screen door, to let some fresh air in. Mother Follic appeared just inside when he got close.

"Mr. Ells. We didn't think you'd make it back in time." She didn't open the screen door or invite him in.

"For a while there, I kinda doubted it myself, Missus Follic." Ells replied as he looked at her with a little curiosity. She wore a much washed house dress, white with faded orange, red and yellow flowers on it. Her face was drawn and thin, like the rest of her, and her eyes said it was hunger that kept her thin, as opposed to exercise. Her sandy blonde hair was scooped back in a pony tail, all except for two little strands at the sides. Ells didn't know what they called those, but he had always thought the effect looked better on women with dark hair. She finally opened the door and stepped out, holding the door open with her body.

"Were you able to find them?" she asked him.

He nodded and slowly swung his pack around off his shoulders. After a quick rummage, he came up with a linen cloth bundle, wrapped up with a bit of twine string. "Wouldn't have dared darken your door again without I had, Missus. Be careful now," he admonished as he handed the package up the steps to her, leaving his pack sitting on the blacktop driveway, "the smaller one's made of glass." She untied the string and began unfolding the cloth. Her hands developed a tiny shake as she folded back the last flap.

From behind Missus Follic, inside the house, came walking a girl. She was thirteen or fourteen, he couldn't remember which, and she was well developed for her age. She gave him a quick smile as he looked at her with more than a little curiosity. She had a well fed look, and looked to have just grown into her body, no longer all knees and elbows, but rightly proportioned and with the flower of youth still in her cheeks. Her sandy blond hair was cleaned and brushed to a high sheen. The boldness of that same youth was in her eyes as she looked right back at him.

"You clean, Mister?" she asked. It took him a moment to figure out she had spoken, and minute more to puzzle out what she meant. He frowned suddenly and caught himself looking skyward. Ells knew others didn't understand about Dad, better not to draw attention to him. Just as he was pulling his gaze back downward a ringing slap was dealt backhand by the Mrs. Follic to her daughter.

"You're thirteen," she hissed. *Thirteen then*, Ells thought, "and a virgin, why do you want to ask a question like that?"

This was no business of his, so Ells elected to preserve his integrity with silence.

Then the daughter replied though, "Only half a virgin, Daddy's seen to that well enough!"

Ells became very still, and Mother Follic turned beady eyes on him, waiting for a reaction. It all made sense now, these people didn't have to look out for or worry about trouble, they had enough right in the home.

Ells kicked open the garage door, and saw only neatly ordered tools and a half-finished rocking chair in the center of the room on some saw horses. No Daddy here, time to move on. Mrs. Follic was putting fluttery hands on him, pulling at his clothes.

She was saying something like, "You musn't believe her, it's her birthday and she just wants attention," and on and on. Ells put one foot in front of the other until he got to the other outbuilding. Inside he could hear noises, so he slowly opened the door and waited for something to happen.

Instead a man's voice called out, "Well? What is it?" The voice was petulant and annoyed sounding. Ells walked in and the owner of the voice was a middle aged man with a slight paunch. He wore an old tattered sweater with a geometric design on it. His sandy blonde hair was combed over to one side to cover up the top of his bald head. He had been sharpening the blades on his manual pushmower, and stood with the whetstone in his hand.

Ells started off by hitting him in the stomach, taking the man's wind away, but after that didn't have any real rhyme or reason and just hit him. Once Mr. Follic was down Ells kicked him in the back, and his hand fell down to the hilt of his machete. He saw movement in the small side window that faced the empty field.

His Dad was there in the clouds, saying, "No son. This work ain't that big," and just like that it was over. Mr. Follic was badly beaten, and it was only now that Ells recalled he had never told the man why. Mrs. Follic was at the door, the package he had given her dropped and forgotten. The can of chocolate cake frosting that made up one half of its contents rolled until it hit the grass and then stopped. The merry twinkle of the glass bottle of Tabasco hot sauce drew the eye as it sat still miraculously unbroken, but Ells didn't have time for that. He went to the shelves that lined the walls of the small building and found his payment, a tin can of bike chain oil.

He walked out of the building towards the house to retrieve his pack. He held the can of oil in his left hand, and the linen cloth Mrs. Follic had dropped in his right. He began carefully wrapping the can and happened to look up at the house while he did. In a second story window stood the daughter, no longer bold or lusting, but afraid. Afraid of him, who once would have lain with him. Ells shrugged and shouldered his pack, glancing up for a last look, but now there was just a sandy blonde boy staring down at him, his eyes making all kinds of promises and threats.

Ells tipped him a saucy salute. "See ya around, kid."

He started down the driveway, putting one foot in front of the other, and listened to his Dad telling him, "No good ever comes from mixing up with someone else's woman, it's a sure way to get the law on you."

He nodded up at the sky and reminded himself to check the yards and sheds on his way out of town for bicycles. A man on the run needs more transportation than putting one foot in front of another, after all.

The Undercastle

Once upon a time, there was a kingdom whose king lived under a hill. His father's fathers had been great friends of the dwarfs, who were now all gone, and they had built for their friend a castle under a hill. The castle was cunningly constructed, in the way of dwarf craftsmen, and suffered only a very little from age and use. Once the dwarf race had all disappeared, the kings under the hill started to become strange. They left their castle less and less, and eventually not at all. The last king under the hill was said to have been versed in dark and terrible magics that he found deep in the forgotten vaults of his ancient castle. His people knew him as King Antilar the Cruel, as his brand of justice often involved the beheading of petitioners to his darkened court. He had no sons nor daughters when he finally let go his miserable life, and he was filled with a great disgust for the kingdom he ruled over. On his deathbed, he cursed the kingdom he was about to abandon and all the people in it.

For their part, the people of his kingdom were largely glad to be rid of such a tyrannical and cruel ruler, curse or no curse. Their lives went on, as lives will, but in a markedly better state without the bands of King's men looking to collect taxes. All of that gave way into lawlessness once news of the King's death spread outside the strange and backwards kingdom of Undercastle. It is known that with the lawless element comes those would make their own laws, and stand up to the worst of the transgressions committed in a kingdom with no King. Four such men arrived on the border of Undercastle fifteen years after the death of King Antilar the Cruel, with a plan to set things right...

The innkeeper set tankards of what he called ale on the table, and the big man growled. The tavern man hunched away, fearful. He didn't know the big man growled when he was happy. The other three men at the table knew, but they didn't care if the innkeeper was scared. In fact, it was likely better for him to be that way. The big man gripped his tankard and drank deep, smacking his lips in satisfaction. Thin or not, he liked his beer. The light, foamy head turned his graying mustache white, and little rivulets trickled down through his thick beard to spatter on the chain link shirt he wore in perpetuity below.

He looked around at his table mates. "Not drinking?" he asked. "This swill barely counts, trust me."

"Not all of us have your refined taste," said the thin man wearing heavy clothing and swaddling furs across from him without looking up from what he was working on, "nor your unconditional love for swill of any stripe." In front of him sat a teapot that he had given arms and legs. He chanted over it briefly and made a few passes with his hands. The limbs he had attached to thing rattled a bit, then lay still. He cursed quietly.

"Still can't get the bugger to walk, eh? Should try offering it a coin or two. Makes the world turn, that does. Could get your little tea man up and about." The lithe man wearing a vest of dirty brigandine alternated poking at his teeth and scraping beneath his permanently dirty fingernails with a sliver of wood as he spoke. While the pick was in his mouth, he buffed his nails on a shirt made from patchwork he wore under his armor.

He stopped and grabbed for his tankard, draining half its contents with convulsive gulps. The man set his mug down. "Blech. That's foul, that is. Reminds me of south kingdoms ales, and that's no good memory, eh lads?"

The last man of the four sat forward and pushed back his hood, revealing a heavily scarred face and blind eyes. "Which trip south, the snakes or the island?" he asked, his hand reaching unerringly for the handle of his tankard.

"Either," came the unanimous reply, "both." The men laughed together, and the innkeeper was set slightly more at ease.

"Aly, bring the stew!" the portly man called, waving his serving girl out of the kitchen. When she walked out to the table, the laughter stopped.

She was beautiful in the way that only something surrounded by ugliness can be, like an apple tree in full bloom on a battlefield or a songbird in a mineshaft. Her skin was moonlight and mahogany, and even with her hair covered with a serving woman's bonnet, the glorious fall of it was gold shot through with obsidian. She carried the four bowls with long practice, and slung them on the table in front of each of the men oblivious to the quiet her arrival had engendered. She gave the men a small smile, crinkling the spray of nearly invisible freckles across the bridge of her nose, and then walked away without a second look at them.

They all looked at each other. Their plan was missing just one crucial element, just one thing more to carry the day. They could get to the castle, infiltrate its depths, and seize the throne. But who would sit it? Who indeed.

Part the First: A Journey to Undercastle

"Sebastian, we haven't had proper tea leaves for weeks, and yet…" The big man was sounding morose, as the ale had run out shortly after the tea.

"And yet, Barlen, I persist. Why? Because, this. Will. Work." Still wearing his thick layer of furs, the thin man known as the Toymaker after his clockwork contraptions made arcane passes over the teapot that he had given arms, legs, and now two garnet eyes. He chanted a sonnet in the language of forests, with some words of crackling fires and blacksmith's anvils thrown in. The little teapot man was motionless.

Sitting next to Sebastian Toymaker, the lithe man spoke up. "Ha, poor little bugger's got the good sense not to work without there's a bit of coin in it. I'd be the same, had I a round little teapot arse."

"I think it's cute. And, when it works? Less fetching and carrying for me. So you just keep on until he's running us all tea and crumpets, Sebastian, and never mind what Dirk says. Not everything is about the getting of riches." Aly had fitted into the group as if they were missing her all along. After just a few days on the road, it was as if she was always there, and her life at the inn was a story that had happened to somebody else.

"Not everything, lass, just the only thing." Dirk grumbled, snatching up a branch to poke the fire with. They had made camp in a clearing in some piney woods, well off the road. In these troubled times, one was often safer away from the road than on it. The fire spit up sparks and snapped at being poked, in the way of knotty pine fires. The last of their number stepped out from the darkness and into the light of the flames.

"We were not followed here," he intoned, leaning easily on the walking stick he carried. Like the man himself, the blind man's stick was unique. When asked, he would say it was made from a plant that grew in the desert, but only just after it rained. After the rain water dried, the plant would hide itself under the sands again, waiting for another shower to emerge again, even if it took years. The wood itself was light as a feather and as hard as iron. Again, somewhat like its owner. "The highwaymen have lost our scent."

"Highwaymen, is it? You make 'em sound lordly, instead of the beasts they is." Dirk said to him. He turned his unseeing eyes toward Dirk. For some, it was unsettling.

"Aye, beasts. Your wound?" In addition to being their scout in the wilds, the blind man was their healer.

"Not more'n a scratch, this. Yon Aly-cat, she put it to rights." Dirk's voice was normally harsh, angry. He couldn't keep the fondness out of it when he talked about the girl, and to her.

"She's got the knack of it, right enough." Barlen rumbled.

Alysanne blushed to be praised. It was part of why they were all growing fond of her. "It's nothing. Just some things P taught me. Now get set here by the fire, mister, and take some supper." She called the blind man P, short for Pariah, which she thought was an awful name for a healer and a seer.

He sat, leaning his staff against his shoulder and stretching his hands toward the fire. The corners of his mouth were just upturned in the barest hint of a smile. "Supper. That would be welcome."

They were all growing fond of her.

The bandits attacked in the night.

Dirk had the watch, and was testing his weighted knuckle bones on a length of split wood when he felt it. It took years of living as they had to register that feeling; the feeling of malice aforethought and murder bent on one person from another. He acted through instinct as much as experience, taking up his long handled hammer and growling a warning to the others. "Up you lazy sods, it's about to be bloody!" He had time to give the huge pile of blankets the Toymaker slept under a kick for good measure and then the enemy was on them. Dirk did for the first of them, letting the bandit cut harmlessly to his right as he swung his hammer down on the other man's skull. Three more followed behind the first, looking to swarm him. "Up, you bastards!" he called.

Barlen, the big man, came up roaring like he always did. Years of sleeping on the road and worse places had trained them all to snap awake ready for action at a moment's notice. He slid his notched old longsword free of its scabbard and put his arm through the loop on his shield as he stood. He stood to Dirk's right, guarding over Sebastian.

The Toymaker struggled up, cursing. He hated to be woken in the night. Nevertheless, long practice had his crossbow at the ready in a breath. He twisted a knob on the side, yanked a lever sticking out of the top and pulled the trigger mechanism while aiming up and away, into the branches. A burst of bright white light shot toward the pine boughs above them, making the clearing and surrounding area as visible as if it were noon instead of midnight. He took one step, moving behind Barlen.

Pariah slept sitting up, with his legs crossed and his staff leaning against his shoulder. In one smooth motion, he stood and gripped the weapon in both hands, ready for what might come. An arrow whistled in, and he knocked it aside. "Alysanne, behind me," he said calmly.

Aly scrambled from her bedroll, yanking a dagger out from under her pillow. Ten men now surrounded the little group in the clearing.

A man wearing oddments of armor and carrying a bearded ax spotted with rust stepped forward, away from the rest of the robbers. "We'll have those weapons and any coin you might be carrying." His eyes lit on Aly, crouched behind Barlen and Dirk with her knife in hand. "Her as well. Long time since we had anything like her out here, eh boys?" The other men shared a chuckle as the hideous smile faded from the face of their leader. "Toss 'em down or we'll have you—" before the man could finish, Dirk swung his long handled hammer, frighteningly fast for such a large weapon. The leader's jaw was broken and dislocated with an audible snap and pop. Barlen brought his shield around, driving the man's body to the ground. Sebastian took careful aim down the length of his crossbow and loosed bolt a that went through the chest of the leader and flipped him onto his back. The bolt buried itself into the bole of a tree up to its feathers with a malignant thrum. Sebastian muttered a few words and twisted a tiny crank on the side of his weapon, and it began the process of reloading itself.

The shock only lasted a moment.

The archers among the robbers opened up, loosing arrows before the charge of the others. Pariah moved like wind over water, knocking the arrows aside as if he knew where they would fly before they were aimed. The six that didn't have bows closed in, with a hodge-podge of dinted and rusted weaponry. One or two carried them with the familiarity of long use and the rest just came on, bloodlust in their eyes.

Barlen charged the encircling line, bellowing from behind his shield. He slammed into the first man he reached, knocking the smaller man flying. The next took the big man's longsword in his skull with a sound like wet wood, splitting. When Barlen swung around to face the next man his opponent was backing away, weapon nearly forgotten in his hands. The bandit never saw the hammer that impacted his temple and sent him spinning to the ground. Dirk wasted no time, but used the momentum from his strike to carry him into the next.

Sebastian's crossbow thrummed again and one of the archers dropped his bow and grabbed at the inch of feathered crossbow bolt that his belly had sprouted. The Toymaker reached into a bag slung over one shoulder and brought out a small brass container that he slapped into the groove where a bolt would normally be placed. He yanked out a cork in the top and breathed a word known by the embers of a fire the morning after it burns out. A gout of flame erupted from the end of his weapon and sprayed two of the men that had advanced to within arm's reach. They fell screaming, rolling on the ground to put out the fire. It didn't help.

Pariah brought down one end of his staff in a whistling blow that stopped the screaming of one of the men. Sebastian slammed his hand against the side his crossbow, and a twelve inch blade slid out of the front end. He stalked forward and stabbed down once, ending the screams.

The two bowmen were now retreating, still loosing shafts, and the lone remaining man turned and ran. Dirk reached for his belt, pulling a hand ax up and looping it in an end-over-end throw, taking the running man in the back.

"Run, you cowards! Run!" Barlen shouted, slamming the guard of his blade against his shield. A cut he had picked up over one of his eyes from somewhere bled freely, giving his face a red mask. Dirk sauntered to the man with the ax in his back and casually pulled it free. He noticed blood running down his fingers and looked at his upper arm, where an arrow had pierced the meat.

"I hate bloody archers," he muttered, snapping off the shaft and pushing the bodkin head of the arrow through to the other side, grunting with pain. "Oi, Pariah! When you've seen to the great lummox, have a look at this, will you?"

Aly was already there, looking the wound over with a critical eye. Her hands only shook a little as she gently probed the edges of the bleeding hole. "It's not bad, Dirk. You were lucky."

He shook his head and laughed. "Luck, lass? Luck is sleeping in a thousand clearings and seeing more'n one of our mates go to the hereafter on account of being slow to wake." He spat to the side. "You make your own bloody luck or you'll have none at all." Then Pariah was there, guiding her movements, his eyes closed as he murmured something low and peaceful. The raw edges of flesh began to knit themselves together.

In a quiet voice, she asked him, "Is it always like this?"

The healer shook his head sadly. "It is usually worse, Alysanne."

Part the Second: Into the Garden

"When I read it described as a hill, I would never have envisioned this." Sebastian said in wonder.

"Hill? That's a damned mountain, that is." Dirk rubbed at his arm, which was still healing. One side effect of Pariah's healing arts was a deep, terrible itch where the flesh was knitting.

Barlen looked at the great rocky mass in front of him, his eyes deep in shadow under his helmet. "Aye, a mountain to us. But just a hill to dwarfs, I'd say."

Behind him, Pariah drew circles in the dirt with the end of his staff, a sure sign he was troubled. "Mountain or hill, men or dwarfs, what we came for is beneath and within."

The girl cleared her throat. "The old stories say that when King Antilar the Cruel died, the entrance to his great hall collapsed on the servants as they tried to escape." Aly had grown more sure of herself after the bandit raid. In truth, she had become more sure of the men she was with. They certainly knew what they were about.

"Not getting in that way, then. The only dwarf I ever knew was overly fond of stonework and secret ways into and out of big stone castles." Barlen stated, stroking his beard.

"But Barlen, sir! The dwarfs are all gone, dead for generations!" Aly blurted in surprise.

Barlen gave her a sidelong glance. He liked to show few enough smarts, but she was learning he had a sharper wit than first glance showed. "Oh, a dwarf will surprise you. And I've no doubt all the dwarf race hereabouts is gone. After all, what use would kings have for them once they got their palace under a mountain?"

Dirk spat and voiced a low chuckle. "None at all, seems to me. Convenient that there aren't any dwarfs left to contradict the stories of their friendship and generosity, innit?"

Sebastian swung his crossbow around, fiddling with a lens he had screwed onto the front sight of the contraption. "Everything appears disturbingly... undisturbed. Aly, can you think of anything else? Any other of those old stories that might hold a clue?"

Her brow furrowed as she mentally sifted through what she knew. Each of the men had had a lot of practice pretending not to watch her being unselfconsciously beautiful. "No..." she said slowly, then, "Wait, maybe. The Boy King, Llewelyn—"

"Pfah!" Dirk grunted a laugh. "You lot named your kings Llewelyn? No great wonder the last one died without spawning!"

"Hush, Dirk." Aly scolded him. Those that knew him knew that a person whom told Dirk to 'hush', learned how quick he was with that hammer of his. Dirk hushed, and Aly went on. "King Llewelyn was once kidnapped by rogues; or was it rebels? The point is, he tricked his kidnappers into carrying him out through the Garden Gate. The Garden Gate opened from the Undercastle onto the royal family's own gardens, which Llewelyn's great-granda Jolly King Daniel had shaped into a hedge maze."

"Gardens need sunshine and rain to grow. Under a mountain, the sun cannot shine and the rain cannot fall. Where are these gardens?" Pariah stood with his face turned to the sky, his staff held at his waist horizontally like a tight rope walker.

Barlen scowled at the densely grown vegetation that looked more like a solid wall than a garden. "You say this was a hedge maze?"

Aly's head bobbed in affirmation. "In the story, the Boy King knew the maze frontwards and backwards, and once he was able to slip his bonds he got his kidnappers so lost they never found their way out."

Barlen slid his longsword free of its scabbard with a whisper of steel on leather and took a swing at the hedge. It stuck fast and yanked him forward, nearly pulling the blade from his grip. He set his feet and heaved the sword free with a terrific screech that sounded as if the thing had been stuck into stone. "Bugger a badger, that thing tried to eat me! What d'yer stories say about that, girl?"

"The castle, the kingdom and all its people were cursed by the last, dying king, Barlen." Sebastian said absently, eying the tall hedge through his lens. "Do you think he spared the family pleasure garden? I think not. Ah! A concealed entrance. Just down this way." The Toymaker motioned with the end of his weapon to a spot on the hedge wall twenty feet to their left.

"Aye, so it is. Here, Barlen, if you're through with the trimming, let's have us through this bloody thing." Dirk stepped through what appeared to be solidly interlocked branches, but was really a pair of swinging doors that had the vegetation weaved into it. Pariah followed him, staff tapping the ground in front of him.

Barlen waved Aly and Sebastian to the door, muttering, "Trimming, is it? Some clever lads could be trimmed by a head or so, not that they'd notice." Aly was sure there was more, but she passed him by, following the Toymaker into the maze.

Aly sighed in exasperation. "We've been past this fountain three times already! The sun's already westering, too."

"Westering? Aly-cat, it's nearly on to bloody dusk. To the side of which, this maze was your idea." Dirk said quietly, which the others knew to be a sign of growing frustration on his part.

"We need to start keeping a map, or blazing our trail, so we know where we've been." she doggedly went on.

Sebastian shook his head in the lengthening shadows, twisting a knob on the side of his crossbow. A tiny light appeared and then traced a turning, twisting line on the ground. "There's our path thus far. We haven't gotten turned around. The other fountains we passed had a statue on the top," he waved briefly at the carved stone. "this one doesn't."

The girl smiled in relief. "No, you're right. I remember thinking how horrid the statue looked, all covered in ivy."

"Nevertheless, this is the same fountain." Pariah said, motioning with his staff to the spot where the statue would have been. In its place were two sets of spade-shaped indents, tipped by three deep claw marks. The other two men readied their weapons, cursing.

Aly's heart jumped into her throat. She fumbled out her knife, trying to look in all directions at once. What she saw was that the four men had automatically made a circle around her. Barlen's low voice rumbled at her, rocks in a tumbler.

"First a shifting maze, and now a gargoyle. I hate gargoyles."

Aly shook her head, and slipped out of the circle between Sebastian and Barlen.

The big man reached for her with his shield arm, missing. "Erg—stay here girl!"

"I'll be fine, we need to—" before she could finish, an icy cold grip with the hard, unyielding strength of stone closed around her wrist. There was an awful pressure, and she could feel the thin bones grinding, one against the other. A breath of air that smelled of pulverized rock and slimy river stones washed over her, and she started to turn to see where that alien stench had come from.

Suddenly, Pariah's stick flashed through her field of vision. There was a thunderous crack, the volume of which made her blink, but the pressure on her wrist did not ease.

"Only one thing for breaking boulders into gravel. Look away, Aly-cat." Dirk's voice was soft, almost loving. Then his long handled hammer whistled down. At the end of his swing, she knew for a fact that the sound she had heard when Pariah had tried to free her was only a small crack, a suggestion of thunder. She screwed her eyes shut and turned her face away as the rock chips began to fly. The grip on her wrist disappeared, and she snatched her hand to her chest as if burned. Barlen was there, his shield arm enveloping her.

"Stay safe, Aly-girl. Without you at the end it's all for naught." he said, the steel of his longsword ringing on stone.

"Another on our right." Pariah said without inflection. Tremors wracked Aly's body once, twice and then she forcibly put aside her fear. It wasn't doing her any good, and it might get her killed. She ignored the shake in her hand as she steadied her grip on her knife and stepped away from the big man. The new enemy had an ugly, twisted, sneering, visage and skin made all over of stone, but was different from the one that Dirk had half-demolished with his hammer in that it was covered in plant growth. A gaping hole in the hedgerow behind it showed where it had been hiding before the ambush. Aly put her other hand on the grip of her blade.

"One side, please." Sebastian's tone was curt, workmanlike. She stepped aside, and the space she had occupied was filled with the red-gold flames that came out of the Toymaker's little brass canisters. The plant growth on the gargoyle's body writhed as it burned, but the creature itself came on, heedless. When it reached for her she slashed at its clawed hand, and she was surprised to see that despite the grating sound of the strike, it opened a shallow wound. The things weren't invincible, just very hard to kill. Pariah stepped in front of her, using his staff to deflect the clawing attacks of the stony monster. Barlen had maneuvered himself around behind the thing, standing in the hole in the hedge wall that it had stood in, and a crunch of gravel accompanied by a soft litany of foul language heralded Dirk's arrival behind her.

Aly was brave, but she knew bravery was not the equal of experience. The four men worked together and quickly reduced the second grotesque to rubble. Pariah laid out a cloth and gathered a pile of the smaller stones.

She started to ask, but she before could frame her question he said, "Trail markers. These creatures were of the maze, and it is my guess that even when inert, their flesh will be unaffected by it."

The small group pushed through past sunset, using torches made from hedge branches for light. It was full dark when they reached the center of the maze, and the moons rode high over head. Once it had been a beautiful topiary garden, with great bushes trimmed into the shapes of all sorts of fantastic beasts. The first thing they noticed when they stepped out from the maze was an overpowering animal stink. Piles of dung littered the stone walkways and where the far exit would have been was a huge tangled pile of dead branches lined inside with leafy green ones, like a massive bird's nest. There were four exits in total, one for each of the four winds; which was only right and proper for a royal hedge maze.

Sebastian said as much as he waved out his torch and tossed it aside. For the first time since entering the maze, the tall hedges weren't obscuring their view of anything but the path ahead, and the Toymaker pointed at the looming mountain, "I hope you're right about this secret door, Aly. I don't favor the idea of climbing around that looking for a way in."

"Alysanne had the right of it about the maze. She'll be right about the door, in time." Pariah poked at one of the dung piles with the end of his stick, dislodging it from the ground and sliding it a few inches. "Dry. Old."

"The stink of it ain't, that's sure. Yonder nest looks to be lived in as well. These queer bushes haven't just growed this way on their own, neither. On your guard gents, m'lady." Dirk gave a complicated tug on the handle of the hammer that stuck up over his shoulder, freeing it from the rig that held it in place. The rest of the group readied their weapons, and they moved together through the moonlit center of the maze, trying to watch all the exits at the same time. The large topiary animals made Aly nervous. Here there was unicorn, there a great standing bear, and all of them looked as if they were leering over the group as they passed, full of silent menace. One in particular, a man with three fingers on each of his outstretched hands and the horned head of a bull on top of his squat, leafy neck drew her gaze again and again, until she finally noticed the gleam of steel beneath the thing's feet. She wandered over, ignoring an impatient hiss from Dirk, and picked up the pair of gardening shears. They were immaculately kept up, sharpened and greased with some foul-smelling unguent. She scissored them, once and again, enjoying the mechanical precision of a well-kept tool.

The high pitched, ear straining sound of an enraged bull shattered the stillness of the night.

The group was caught in the middle of the clearing when the tangled nest burst apart, and stomping through the detritus was the twin of the hedge creature that Aly stood before. He, and he was unmistakably male, was taller at the shoulder than Barlen was at the top of his head. The great bull's head looked down on them with glowing red eyes. He roared again, and snorted steaming air from his nostrils.

Two more shrieking roars answered, each from other exits to the maze. The heavy clopping of hooves signaled their attack.

Barlen set his shield and feet to receive the charge of the third beast to show itself, and Pariah stood just to his side, ready to to foul the thing's footing with his staff and bring it to the ground. Sebastian said a few words that sounded like a clock's ticking as he manipulated the limbs of his crossbow into the device and twisted knobs along its length. When he was finished, a metal ball the size of a fist shot from the end of his weapon in a short arc. Before it could hit the ground, its surface folded open into a myriad of sharpened edges, interspersed with spikes. The ball began to fly of its own accord, directly into the face of the second beast. Dirk's charge carried him right behind the Toymaker's attack, his hammer making meaty impacts against the monster's body.

The first creature narrowed his red eyes at Aly and pawed the ground with one hoof. He dropped into a three point stance with the ease of long practice.

Before he could start his charge, Aly commanded, in a voice she hardly recognized as her own, "Stop! I demand that you stop this!" She raised the shears, sliding them open and placing the edges along the neck of the topiary minotaur in front of her.

Everything stopped.

The three monsters looked frozen in place, their glowing red eyes wide with fear. The two later arrivals snorted and gave out a lowing, questioning moan, and their leader responded by standing to his full height and spreading his arms wide in an obvious show of nonaggression.

"Let us pass and no harm will befall your maze! Show us the way to the door, and I will return your shears." Aly shouted to the monsters. The only reply was a single, sharp snort from the largest one that sent the others backing away into the maze whence they had come.

"Dangerous gamble, Aly-girl." Barlen rumbled at her as he backed to her position. "Lucky it worked."

"Not so dangerous if you know the tale, Barlen. King Antilar cursed all in his kingdom when he died, his magnificent Undercastle and its servants most of all." Aly tapped him on the shoulder and pointed towards the minotaur with the shears. "Those are what's left of the royal gardeners charged with keeping this maze."

"Your tales tell you all that, Aly? I think not. An ingenious leap of logic," Sebastian said as he waved the ball he had summoned back to him. When it reached his strange crossbow, it disassembled into various components that integrated themselves with the mechanism. "No doubt when you saw the care with which they kept this," he indicated the topiary, "and those," the shears, "you made the connection. Astute."

"Aye, astute. And if you trust that bloody monster not to slaughter us the minute he's got his shiny bit back, you're more a fool than that old dead king," Dirk said, his weapon still in his hands. "Off with us to the secret garden door."

The minotaur's heavy tread and breathing drowned out any other night sounds the maze might have held, and in less than half the time it had taken them to reach the center, he lead them to an unremarkable slab of mountain stone. The animal reek of him was stronger even than the pervasive smell of dung from the maze's center. Judging from his physical reaction to Aly, it had been some time since the minotaurs had captured their last female.

"This is it? Right, I'll have a look. The rest of you keep an eye out for this bugger's mates." Dirk began a close inspection of the wall, using his fingers and nose as much as his eyes. "Ah, I've a seam here, but no way in yet..."

Behind him, the bull-headed monster blew hot breath through its nose and put one massive three-fingered hand in the center of the door, exerting steady pressure. With an enormous scraping sound of stone against stone, the rough-hewn shape of the door revealed itself as it slid backwards into the mountain.

Aly stepped to the beast, holding the shears before her. The massive, shaggy head of the thing dipped, the great spread of his horns wider than Aly's arms could reach from tip to tip. She offered the clippers to the beast, holding one of the handles so he could grip the other. He put one had on the shears, bunching his other into a tight fist. His wide, red eyes slitted down to glowing lines.

Dirk's hammer crunched into the top of the monster's horned head, and the monster dropped like a puppet with its strings cut, all in heap. "Thanks for upsy-daisy, big fella."

Barlen pushed himself to his feet; he had knelt to catapult Dirk into the air. "Had to be done, Aly-girl. Couldn't walk into the Undercastle with that thing behind us," he said to the glare Aly was giving him.

"Aye, might as well slit our own bloody throats here and now and be done with it as leave this big bugger behind us, bull head full of how to get back at us." Dirk gave the big monster another shot, this one behind one of the creature's floppy bovine ears.

"Stop it! P! Make him stop!" Aly screamed.

Pariah stood as he had, unseeing eyes scanning the inky dark that the opened door had revealed. "We could sooner stop the tide as what must be. To avoid reprisals from this poor wretch's clan, we ought leave the shears."

She turned, tears in her eyes, to the Toymaker. "Sebastian, please."

He was busy examining the secret door. "Hm? Oh. They're right, Aly. Nothing for it but to move on. Fascinating construction here…"

After hesitating the space of a few breaths, she scrubbed away her tears and followed the four men under the mountain.

Part the Third: The Burden of Service

"These tunnels might have been dug with giants in mind! Abnormal for dwarf stonemasons, I assure you. No truer enemies than the dwarf and giant races." Sebastian's commentary had been more or less constant since leaving the hedge maze behind.

"They were built for men. This whole place was meant for men," Aly said flatly. The group's betrayal of the minotaur had changed something between them. Dirk had been silent, watching her carefully. She could feel his eyes, and the others' as well occasionally. The small tunnel from the doorway had opened up wider and wider, until the small light that Sebastian's magic conjured no longer revealed either wall, nor the roof.

"So it was, Aly. How clever of you to remember! Look just there, it's…" Sebastian was babbling, his reaction to the unease in the air.

"Enough, Toymaker. We'll have quiet, I think." Barlen belied the harsh feel of his words with a friendly hand on the other man's shoulder.

Sebastian fell silent, and it wasn't any better.

The sound of their footfalls echoed in the large chamber, seeming to redouble as they bounced around, until it sounded like an army's marching. The meager light revealed stone steps, shallow and wide. They were covered in ruined furniture and strange, rusted iron spikes. It came to Aly in a flash of intuition.

"A music hall!" she said in delight. "The tunnel would have

focused the music out into the gardens." She pointed at the stone work and wrecked furniture. "There's where the band would sit. But look, so many seats!"

"An auditorium, with seating for an orchestra. It would seem your kings of old did not dream small, Alysanne." Pariah had moved with his customary fluidity, seemingly not even disturbing the dust beneath his sandals. "We should search for the band's entry point. It is likely concealed and hopefully overlooked as unimportant by the last king when he brought down the mountain in his death throes."

Dirk nodded, finally taking his eyes away from Aly. "Aye, I'll have a look. You lot stay here. No heroics without me, yeah?" He moved out of the light cast by the globe that bobbed above Sebastian's head, his hammer over one shoulder. She turned her back on him.

"It wasn't right," she said sotto voce as soon as he was out of sight, "we had a compact with them."

Barlen flinched from her tone, and heaved his shoulders in a sigh. "Think back, Aly-girl. What did you see?"

Instead, she bunched up her hands and shook her head, "It's not right!"

Pariah stepped in front of her, cracking her knuckles with his staff. "You are seeing what you wanted to see. Think back to what you observed."

She stopped, rubbing her knuckles. She thought about the hand reaching for the shears. She remembered what the thing's other hand had been doing. She thought about the gleaming red eyes of the minotaur and his obvious arousal.

Sebastian could see the realization come over her. "He would have knocked you senseless and killed us if he could. After we were dead, he would have carried you back to his sculpted garden to make more gardeners, until you died of it. I'm sorry," he said, meaning more what she had lost than what the men had done.

"It could not have ended any other way." Pariah agreed, solemn.

Dirk stepped back into the light. "Here, I've found the path." He looked into Aly's eyes, and she stared back levelly. He nodded, satisfied.

"Show me the way," she said.

Behind the risers in the amphitheater, a small concealed entrance led to a room lined with wardrobes and storage cabinets. Drums, strings, woodwinds and various other musical instruments littered the room, each badly decayed by the passage of long years. The group moved quietly into the room, Barlen bringing up the rear. Dirk was already scouting for the next doorway.

"Got to be one, lords and ladies hate seeing the serving people come and go. Prefer 'em to appear like bloody magic and disappear as quick when they ain't needed, they do." he muttered as he searched. The others stood in the center of the room, ill at ease with the ruined finery all around them.

A cymbal crashed to the ground in the corner of the room Dirk stood in.

Sebastian whistled between his teeth and silence reigned almost immediately. "Quietly, Dirk my old friend," he said when the effect had run its course.

"I didn't bloody touch the thing, Toymaker. Fell over on its own without help from any of us." He took a small flask of oil from his belt and worked it into the hinges of one of the wardrobe doors and grumbled to himself. "'Quietly', he says. As if I don't know the how of being quiet." One of the biggest drums, a monstrosity that would take two strong men to shift, began to thump in a regular beat. "Now that's definitely not me! Toymaker, shut that racket, can you?"

Sebastian whistled again, but this time the noise did not stop. Thump-thump. Thump-thump. Thump-thump, went the big drum, sounding like a mammoth heart beating. The pipes, fifes and brassy instruments began trilling and blowing randomly, followed closely by the strings. It sounded like an orchestra tuning up, all noise with no direction. The music should have been impossible given the ruined state of the instruments, and on it went.

"Weapons then, lads," Barlen said, matching action to words as he loosed his longsword, "and be quick about it. We don't want everything in this blasted hole to hear the fanfare." He stepped toward the string section, raising his blade to strike at one of the impossible, animated violins. The bow stopped its movement across the strings and pointed itself at him. He stopped in surprise and it went back to its business.

"Wait." Aly said, motioning downward with her hands. "Just wait. For all we know, this is supposed to happen. Keep looking for the way out, Dirk!" she called. Then the music started.

It was a dirge, music that started soft and slow, just the strings humming. The biggest horns sounded out, long and low. The giant drum sounded just once, signaling the arrival of the winds as they keened alongside the low thrum of the strings. After a few moments, the drums sounded again, thumping an irregular rhythm. The high strings added their voices to the winds, wailing like pained, living things. Aly felt wetness on her face and was surprised to find tears streaming down when she raised her hand to wipe it away. The big man snuffled next to her. Sebastian lowered his crossbow and wiped at his eyes with a sleeve. She watched as Dirk tore a length of cloth from the edge of a handkerchief and then tore the strip in half, stuffing the results in his ears. Pariah stood silent, his eyes closed and staff held upright in front of him. The music played on, a requiem meant only for the ears of the dead. Aly barely noticed lying down. She was so tired, so very tired. Why hadn't she noticed it before? They all needed rest.

She came awake when something rapped against the bridge of her nose hard enough to make starbursts form across her vision.

"This is no music, Alysanne. It is an assault!" Pariah helped her to stand and waved her to the other two. "Get them up. I will deal with this."

Aly went to the prone shape of Barlen, shaking him, trying to wake him. Behind her, Pariah began chanting, his voice a drone that bled over and cut through the music. Barlen wasn't waking up. His eyes fluttered, but he slept on, ensorcelled by the dead orchestra. Finally she drew her knife and laid the pommel of it against his helm, making it ring. He struggled upright, shaking his head. Pariah's voice grew in intensity, the volume of it seeming to bubble up from under the funereal orchestra and flood over it. The words he chanted over and over must have been a mantra, they had form and structure but Aly was at a loss to their meaning. They seemed to run in a circle, always coming back to a humming sort of 'aum.'

Dirk kicked through one of the wardrobe doors he had been working on, staving it in. He yanked the remnants out of the way and peered inside. The drum mallet took him in the back of the head, sending him staggering through the secret exit.

A flute bent itself over the rim of Barlen's shield as he held it over Aly, who was crouched next to Sebastian, trying to wake him.

Pariah stood his ground, his droning chant now the only thing that was audible in the chamber. The half-rotted body of a great cello hurled itself at him, and he sent it crashing away in a jumble of splinters and strings. The bow, the real threat to begin with and concealed by the larger piece, grazed his cheek as he just avoided it going into one of his blind eyes. When it swung around for another blow, he deftly swatted it away; breaking its back. He moved to the rhythm of his chanting, swaying like a flag in the desert breeze, rippling like a river in flood. At first he simply avoided the attacks of the instruments. More and more were flying at him and the disciplined, contained energy of his movements lashed out, sending them away broken and useless.

The Toymaker sat up, levering himself quickly up to his feet. "Where's Dirk?" he shouted over his compatriot's chanting. Aly looked around and did not see the slim figure of Dirk anywhere. One of the wardrobes was smashed in, and another was simply open, showing an empty interior.

"Maybe there!" she said, pointing. She hadn't needed to shout, she realized. The chanting had stopped between breaths with a final reverberating 'aum' and when it was gone, so was the terrible, eerie music. Pariah had stopped moving as well, his chest heaving in and out as he stood crouched with staff held in one hand and his feet spread wide. He breathed in through his nose and out through his mouth in steady, controlled sequence. Gradually he slowed until his breath was quiet and even.

"Are you well, P?" Aly asked him, worried. She had never seen him show the slightest sign of effort when he fought in the past.

He straightened, leaning on his staff. His normally ageless face looked somehow older, drained. "As well as one such as I can be Alysanne. No worse and no better. Let us seek out Dirk. He would not have left us willingly."

He stood in the center of the room, the head of his hammer chalked white by the blows against the skeletal creatures that now lay scattered around him. His face was a mask of blood, and two long, red furrows ran back from over his left eye into his black hair. He looked up at them when they burst into the room, saying only "Took you lot long enough to get here," before he collapsed.

Sebastian held up a skull from one of the things that Dirk had destroyed. It was strangely bird-shaped; round in back and tapering down to a bony beak, with eye sockets that seemed small in comparison to the dimensions of the rest of the features. "They stood twice as tall as a man, you say?"

"Aye, twice as tall and twice as wide at the shoulder, if I'm any judge." He sucked in a breath in pain; Aly stood over him as he sat, working at his wound. "Careful Aly!" Dirk had nodded his head without thinking, but Aly didn't mention it. She kept on stitching.

Barlen held up one of the claws that tipped the skeletal creatures' hands. "These are no laugh, either." It was bigger than Aly's knife, and still wickedly sharp.

"D'ya see me laughing, big man? Buggers had four of 'em on each hand, two over and two under. One of 'em came at me from behind, burst up out of the ground, like, and damn near took the eye. His underneath claws hooked into me armor. Only reason he didn't pick me up and tear me limbs off was his grip slipped," he barked a harsh laugh, "slipped through my scalp! Fie, girl!" he yelped in pain as Aly's needle slipped again. This time it had been her fault, she had flinched at his dispassionate description of his narrow escape.

She took a deep breath to steady her hands, as P had taught her. Pariah himself stood off to one side, his hood up and hiding his face in shadows, as it had since leaving the orchestra practice chamber.

"So you got hit from behind and woke up with one of these," Barlen motioned to the scattered bones on the floor, "dragging you here?"

"More like it was dragging me somewhere. My waking up and taking a swing at one of its spindly legs might've cocked up the plan, like." This time Dirk kept his head still. He rolled his eyes up, trying to make contact with Aly. "You through yet, Aly-cat? I've about had enough, if it's torture you had in mind."

She pulled the last stitch tight and tied it off, stepping back from him. "Done." she said, looking again at the hooded blind man. "P?"

Under his hood, his head moved slowly left, then right. "I regret that I cannot. Fighting the force in the music was not simply a matter of the body. It... Tired me more than I thought."

Dirk raised his hands to pick at his scalp, and Aly absently moved them away, most of her attention on trying to get a glimpse of the face under the hood. "Figures," the wounded man said, "it's always been my portion to suffer."

Sebastian had laid out as complete a skeleton as remained, showing the truth of Dirk's words. Its limbs were long, and its frame wide. "Aly, do you know what these were?"

"It could be... They could be the King's visitants. It was said that so just was the rule of the first King of Undercastle that strange beings from far over the ocean came to treat with him. They were said to have strength and speed beyond the capabilities of men, and they were wise in the way of kingship. It is told that they could turn invisible at will and only the whistling wings of a startled dove could reveal them. But..." She trailed off, uncertain.

Pariah spoke from the darkness under his hood. "But what, Alysanne? These Kings of Undercastle came to a bad end. Surely their trusted advisers tried to help them."

"They did, but... Only the oldest stories tell of the wisdom of the visitants. Most tell about how they were feared, using their strange powers to enforce the King's laws at every hearth. 'Speak not ill of the king, lest his ears be near' is a common saying in our kingdom." She stopped suddenly, and looked down at the skull. She half-sang, half-recited in the quiet:

"Eyes are nearly blind,

but heard are words of kin and kine

sent are the disloyal

before the judgment royal,

until our end

until our end

Until the end of them."

They left the remains of the visitants behind without saying another word.

The squared-off room with the scattered and pulverized bones had only one way forward, which led to a long hall with walls that had beds every two strides or so.

"A dormitory? A barracks?" Sebastian thought aloud. "So many beds. Very little luxury here."

Dirk, in the lead, spoke up. "Servant's quarters, most like. I'm surprised we ain't run across the kitchens yet. Royalty likes to have the sweet cakes and such near to hand when music's in the offing. Must've staged the food in the minstrels' practice room for their outdoor parties." He kicked over a basket, tumbling out two large mold colonies and sending up a cloud of spores.

Aly recognized the color and strong smell of the fungus. "That was bread, once. Strange..."

"Aye, Aly-girl. Why weren't the rats at it?" Barlen crouched over the lumps reaching one big paw out, until Dirk slapped it away.

"Oi! Because it's poison, ye great daft fool! Have the sense of a rat and don't touch it."

Barlen yanked his hand back and stood quickly, brushing imagined flecks of mold from his byrnie. "Poison in the bread. Foul!"

Sebastian leveled his crossbow and loosed another ball of light that floated down the length of the corridor-like room until it hit the opposite wall and stuck there, just above the lintel of a door. "We should move on." he said.

The long dormitory let into a small mud room, and some of the pegs around the walls still had mouldering cloaks hanging from them. The small group walked into the room guided by Sebastian's light.

Aly kicked clinging mud from her boots. "Ugh. Water must be seeping up from under the mountain. Let's get to the door, and out of here."

"Small problem, lass." Barlen had sunk up to his knees in the sticky morass, and his struggles to free his legs only sank him deeper.

The Toymaker folded the limbs of his weapon back out, and then folded out two more from the stock. He held it in front of him and spoke words that would have sounded at home in the mouths of hummingbirds. A blue white energy filled the circle created by the rounded limbs on either end of the device, and then he dropped it.

The glowing blue bow stopped a few inches above the surface of the mud, hovering there. Sebastian stepped onto it lightly and moved to the center of the room, where Barlen was now mired up to his waist. Aly stayed back by the door, and Dirk was moving around the perimeter of the room by swinging from peg to peg. Pariah backed away from the door, back into the dorms, readying himself for a single long jump that would carry him over the mud.

Several things happened at once. The peg Dirk was hanging from snapped off, dropping him arse first into the mud. Sebastian and Barlen grabbed each others' arms and as the floating disk began to rise, Barlen began to be freed. Then the mud rose up, first as two thick arms. Then a crude head with the rudiments of a face emerged, centered by a gaping mouth. Aly turned and ran.

"Blue buggery muddy bastard!" Dirk shouted, scrambling to his feet and loosing his hammer.

Barlen came free of the mud, nearly sending himself and Sebastian over the other side of the disk. The Toymaker trilled a word and the disk spread to a width that caught them both before they hit the mud.

Pariah ran and leapt, only instead of clearing the breadth of the room, his momentum carried him directly at the mud-thing, delivering a terrific kick to the center mass of it. His leg sank in up to the hip, and the thing laughed a thick, burbling, horrific laugh as it wrapped its arms around him.

Dirk swung his hammer from his position behind the thing, sending gobs of thick mud splattering against the walls and making rents in the body of the monster that filled in as soon as they appeared. Barlen and Sebastian had gained their feet on the platform and the big man had drawn his blade and was holding it with both hands, leaving his shield slung on his back.

"Closer," he rumbled, not daring to step back into the slimy muck. Sebastian pushed his hands forward, and the disk slid smoothly through the air to put his friend into striking distance. Barlen swung his longsword in great, sweeping strokes that did more to endanger the rapidly disappearing Pariah than to damage the mud-thing.

"Oi!" Aly shouted, unconsciously mimicking Dirk, "Hungry? Eat this!" Her arms were loaded with baskets from the dorm, each one with great lumps of mold growing in them. She hurled them at the monster, laughing. The baskets that landed in the muck sank quickly, but she landed one directly in the maw of the monster.

Its rudimentary lips turned downward into an almost comic

frown as it involuntarily swallowed the poisoned lump in its throat. It loosed its hold on Pariah, folding its thick arms into its mouth, reaching far down its muddy gullet, trying to save itself.

Sebastian reached into his mud spattered and bedraggled furs, coming out with a heavy lead flask that he carefully uncorked and poured into the muck under the disk. The mud began to dry and crack, and then harden. The toymaker calmly said, "Best not to be in contact with it when it spreads."

Barlen dropped his sword onto the disk at his feet and reached for Pariah, pulling him free easily now that the mud-thing wasn't actively holding him. Dirk jumped for the pegs that had previously supported him, spreading his weight across several by hooking the long handle of his hammer over them and hanging from the ersatz bar.

It took only seconds for the mud to turn all to stone, freezing the monster in mid-convulsion.

"I thought you'd turned tail and run, m'lady!" Dirk boomed, beaming at Aly. She blushed involuntarily, making the blushing worse by disliking the blushing.

"Aye Aly-girl, that was some quick thinking! Well done!" Barlen stepped carefully off the disk, clearly mistrusting it now that the danger was over. Pariah only nodded, busily clearing mud from his nose and mouth.

"Sorry I didn't use that sooner, fellows. I couldn't be sure of what we faced until it revealed itself, and then I was loathe to take the chance while it had one of our own." The Toymaker stepped off the disk and began the process of turning it back into the more familiar configuration of his crossbow.

Part the Fourth: The Undercastle

The mud room of the dormitory exited to the courtyard of the Undercastle. There was a hush over the group as the silence of ages weighed down upon them. The building they left behind turned out to be just a small outlier to the main palace itself. Light filtered down from six shafts above that reached all the way to the surface. Beneath each stood a tree; their dead, skeletal branches stretching up to the light. The courtyard stretched away to their right and left, and the left was blocked by an old landslide of boulders twice the size the inn Aly had grown up in.

On their right stood the Undercastle, massive and brooding. It was surrounded by a moat that flowed with the waters of river that had never seen the sky; the moat bridged by a length of stone carved to look like two extended arms gripped in a handshake, symbolizing friendship between the men and dwarfs that had created the cavern and the castle within it. Beyond the bridge was the Undercastle. It was made in the way of dwarf castles everywhere, but at twice the size to accommodate the men that would live in it. Heavy square cornered stone walls stood in three recessing tiers, the topmost being a castle in its own right with soaring twin crenellated turrets that left just enough space between the tops of the merlons and the roof of the huge cavern for a man to stand.

The Undercastle walls had only three sides, because the rear wall consisted of the back of the cavern itself. The bottom tier had but one sally port, wide enough to allow four ox-drawn wagons at one time. The great stone doors stood ajar.

"Looks clear." Dirk said in a monotone voice. The men shared a look and then broke out into laughter. "Bloody castle isn't getting any closer."

"Aye, let's leg it." Barlen swung his shield around and moved carefully into the city-sized space. The others followed, each in a high state of awareness. Still, the trees took them by surprise.

A huge ripping and snapping sound broke the unnatural silence of the courtyard as the trees uprooted themselves and moved to the attack. They were huge, with boles so large all five of them standing in a circle around one would not be able to touch hand to hand. "Run. Run!" Barlen shouted, suiting action to words and making for the bridge. The trees began pulsing with a strange eldritch light as they closed in on the running group.

Then Pariah stumbled, and fell.

"Up, man!" Dirk yelled as he shot past at a sprint. Sebastian spared not a word, his attention consumed with alterations he was making to his weapon on the fly. Aly stopped and pulled at his arm, dragging him to his feet.

She meant to encourage him to keep running but what she saw when his hood fell back took her breath away. In the space of a few hours, he had aged into an old man. He placed one palsied hand over hers and gently removed it from his arm.

"Go," he said, "go, and leave me Alysanne. I cannot run any longer, but I will hold them as long as I am able."

"no" she whispered.

"Yes," he gave her slight push. "Now go. Go!" He turned his back on her, swinging his staff in slow arcs as the branches started to reach for him.

She turned and ran.

Barlen and Dirk stood to either side of the bridge, their hands on great levers.

"Pariah?" Dirk yelled at her.

She shook her head. Dirk grimaced and and Sebastian took

one automatic step back toward the bridge. "He's giving us the chance to finish this, Toymaker. So let's have it finished." Barlen growled.

"What are you doing?" Aly shouted.

"If I'm right, these levers will draw the bridge and keep those things on the far side of the moat." Sebastian explained, his mind back on the turning of gears and manipulation of machinery.

"And trap P on the other side! We can't do this!" she grabbed the Toymaker's arm and shook him out of his reverie. He only stared blankly back at her.

"He'll die!" Aly screamed in his face.

"On three big man. And it's one. Two. Three!" Dirk and Barlen pulled the levers, which moved with a squeal of protest at first but then smoothly slid back. The two interlocking hands came apart, each moving back and away from the other until the bridge was no more, and the halves it lay flush against opposite sides of the bank.

"He'll die." Aly said, to no one in particular. She stared at the tight grouping of witched trees that thrashed in a nonexistent wind.

Dirk turned her away from the courtyard and toward the Undercastle. "There's no help for it, m'lady. It had to be done. Pariah himself would say—"

She dashed silent tears away from her face with one hand and shrugged off Dirk's grip. "It could not have ended any other way. Let's go."

Barlen and Sebastian cast one lingering glance back at the violently thrashing trees, and then followed after the other two.

Inside the great stone doors, a great entry hall lined on either side with stone pillars that reached from ceiling to floor greeted them with the rustle of moth-eaten fabric and the scrabbling of tiny claws. Hung between each of the pillars were banners, once proud and brightly colored. Now, they were drab things, their reds paled to pinks, their whites turned to a foul gray blooming with rot, gold edging split and fraying into a thousand thousand loose threads. At the other end stood another set of stone doors, but these were closed tight. The light from the courtyard gave the area by the doors some small illumination, but as the group edged forward, iron sconces set at the foot of each pillar burst into ghostly blue flame that gave no heat. The doors at the other end of the entry hall were carved in a relief of an empty throne with a crown on its seat flanked by two of the towering visitants, each with one clawed hand on the intricately carved cresting of the royal seat. Unlike the outer doors, these were closed fast. Dirk began examining the carvings and construction minutely, while Sebastian and Barlen took up guard positions on either side.

Aly took a deep breath, and felt it hitch in her chest. She pushed down her emotions, they were here to change everything, and there was no time. Beyond this door was the throne room, the room where Cruel King Antilar had breathed his last foul breath in the form of a curse and left the kingdom without a monarch. She stepped up to the door to try to help, but whatever Dirk was doing worked, and they swung open at her approach.

"Quick work, Dirk. Couldn't have done it better myself." Sebastian complemented his friend as he took a backward step through the door. Beyond, it was deepest darkness. No light penetrated the inky well of the throne room.

"I didn't do a bloody thing." The lithe man muttered in reply, his voice almost below the level of hearing. Barlen turned on his heel, but slow, too slow.

A skeletal hand set with two long, many-jointed fingers over and under and bearing wickedly sharp claws flashed out and gripped the rim of his shield, tearing it away as if the thick leather straps that held it to his arm were made of gossamer. He fended off the second blow with his longsword, only just.

The Toymaker didn't bother to turn, instead firing his crossbow off-bore. The glowing missiles that shot from the end of his weapon arced back around him, and lit brief inroads inside the royal chamber.

The moving, creaking bones of the visitants filled the throne room from end to end and seated on the throne itself was the corpse of the king, crown still on his decayed head.

Aly stood in the doorway, transfixed. A ball of light floated into the room at a few hushed words from Sebastian. The three men waded into the room, laying about with hammer, sword and spell, shattering the horrid bones of the strange creatures. Sebastian finally pulled the trigger mechanism on his crossbow to no result and extended the blade to fight hand to hand, Dirk took a wound, and then another and then a third, and then he called to Aly. "M'lady!" When she made no sign of having heard him, he shouted again, "Aly-cat! The crown!"

Barlen stood back to back with the Toymaker and cut down the visitant in front of him. "Aye Aly-girl, while there's still time!"

Aly watched Sebastian parry an incoming claw with his fantastic weapon and grimace with the effort. "Quickly, Aly, or it will all have been for nothing!"

She walked forward through the fighting as if in a trance. One of the skeletal creatures rattled towards her, clawed hands reaching. Dirk was there, barreling into the flank of the grotesquely tall and spindly bones, knocking them flying. He stalked forward alongside her, blood running freely from his wounds as he drove the bones of the visitants away. The two became encircled. Even with Dirk whirling and slamming his hammer into anything that got too close, the claws came for them.

Barlen slammed through the circle, one of the horridly

elongated rib cages of the visitants threaded over his left arm as a makeshift shield. He walked backwards, fending off attacks from the rear. Aly had eyes only for the dead king on his throne. He seemed almost to be bowing to her as she approached, his peeling skull tipped forward down by the weight of the crown. A clawed hand caught in her hair, cruelly twisting and yanking her out from the shelter of her protectors.

A great bronze hand reached out for the bony arm behind the claw that held her, its plated surface turning with gears and making busy clacking sounds. The Toymaker closed his hand inside the gauntlet he'd formed out of his crossbow, crushing the bones to powder. He stepped to Aly's side, interposing his armored arm and crushing with the augmented strength of his hand.

Aly walked forward a step, and then another, and her hand rose, just a breath away from the crown. This close, she could see that what she took for a simple golden circlet was actually two metals. Gold and something silvery wound around each other and seemed to move like a living thing in the uncertain light cast by the floating globe and marred by the shifting shadows of the battle.

Her fingertips brushed the metal and the king below turned to dust in a susurration of whispers that all had the taste of apologies.

She caught the crown easily and raised it above her head with both hands. Confidently, she lowered it.

The sensation of a deep intake of breath spread inward from the edges of the kingdom and flowed toward the Undercastle and the new Queen.

In the hinterlands, a shepherd turned the tide against a pack of wolves, his arms surging with a newly found strength.

In the garden maze, two bull-headed monsters' shapes twisted as they regained their humanity.

In the courtyard, the trees slowly shifted back to their planters, climbing back up to their ancient homes as tiny leaf buds began to sprout. A man coated in red sat motionless in the lotus position where they had been centered, an old piece of wood broken on the ground before him.

In the throne room, the bones of the visitants fell lifeless in heaps, and Queen Alysanne smiled. The three men, bloodied and beaten, fell shakily to their knees.

"My Queen," swore Barlen.

"Queen Alysanne of the Undercastle," seconded Sebastian.

"M'lady," said Dirk, glancing up to catch her eye and give her a smile. Even through the blood, it was a good smile.

She waved them up. "Rise. It is due to you the curse on the kingdom is lifted. You always believed it was in us, and now we find it to be true."

Neighbors on Briar Creek Road

Pus Ug's daddy was the meanest old bastard that ever lived on Briar Creek Road. Momma doesn't like it when I use words like bastard, but she called Daddy Ug that plenty, so I figure I can too. My name's Charlie, and I live with my brother and sissa and momma and daddy on Briar Creek Road, just up from the Ugs.

Pus never got to school regular, and when he did he always forgot to bring his books so he had to share, and he didn't wash but once every two months, even though he lived right by Briar Creek, just like us.

"I had to slop them hogs," he'd say, or "Daddy said I got to get an ettakayshun so's I ain't a damn fool no more," or he'd just show up with big black eyes or walking with a powerful limp. Pus got picked on by the bigger kids, owing to how skinny and weak he was. He tried to fight back against them kids, but he never won. One day I told my momma how I got a good kick in Pus's ribs when another fella pushed him down and she slapped my face. She told me how I ought act more Christian to those that can't do for themselves. I ran with the story to my daddy, and he boxed my ear one for good measure.

"Your momma's right, boy." he told me. "Now get on and see to the weeds in the garden."

I went. In the next week at the schoolhouse, I left Pus Ug alone, and saw that the kids beating up on him really weren't any better'n he was. The one who beat up on him most was the Buford boy. 'Bufords alias did grow 'em big,' daddy'd said, 'but around here we grow 'em smart. Ain't no child of mine gonna be sharecroppin' the rest of their lives.' Daddy knew about these things, 'cause the Buford boy was big, and not saying anything about my smarts, but that Buford boy was dumb as a post. Seemed he'd beat up on Pus Ug whenever Pus'd speak up in class about knowing his letters or so forth. On a Tuesday, I'd had enough of that.

"Lookit Ug, he's got to roll in the dirt to get clean! Haw-haw-haw!" Buford had Pus Ug pushed down on the edge of the schoolhouse's little garden, holding him there with a big foot on his chest.

"Buford, you leave Ug alone!" I hollered at him. Even as I was saying it, I couldn't believe I was sticking up to Buford, and for Pus Ug! I didn't even like Ug.

"What's it to ya, Irish?" Buford asked me. They called all us kids that, Irish, on account of our name being Maclellan, even though daddy said the fambly came from Scotsland years and years ago. I may not be Buford big, but I got a big fight in me. Momma said it was on account of Scotsland, but I don't know.

"Yer a dunce, Buford, that's what." Well, it was started now. I looked around for any help, but all the kids that were left were standing around by Buford.

"Come over here and say that, Irish. I'll knock you into next week!" Buford wasn't in any hurry to start nothing. Missus Holloway, the schoolmarm, had told him to cut out the fighting or he'd be unwelcome.

"I'd come over there if'n I could stand the smell of you,

Buford! Yer folks got a new kind of washing from the heathens?" Everyone knew Indians smelt the worst. It was a fact.

Well, Buford came for me instead. Him and his buddies, they put a whippin' on me like they meant it for Ug. After, Ug came over and sat by me.

"You all right?" he asked.

"I been whipped proper, Ug. I'll be all right some other time." It wasn't the kindest thing I could've said, but it was the kindest thing I'd ever said to him.

He looked at me puzzled like. His face was all screwed up under the ever-present layer of dirt, like he was thinking hard. Up close, he didn't look so bad. We allas called him pig face and so forth but really, he just looked like a dirty kid. "Why'd you do it, then? You musta knowed you was in for a whippin'."

That right there was a good question. I was surprised even when I was doin' it. I guess that boxin' daddy'd gave my ear must of stuck. "Doesn't seem right, is all." I mumbled. The aches were starting to kick in. I shifted, sore and wanting to get home. Ug stood up and offered me a hand. I needed it. We walked home together on Briar Creek Road, where we was neighbors.

Pus Ug started spending more time around our place, helping me with my chores and practicing numbers with sissa. He was a sharp one for numbers, was Ug, better'n me with 'em by a long chalk. He taught sissa decimals and even fractions, which may as well have been the secret language of Scotsland for all of me. Daddy smiled to see us together, chattering like magpies as we carried the water or split the kindling.

About once a week, Pus Ug's mean old daddy'd come down Briar Creek Road to collect his boy, cursing up a storm about sloth and whippings to be received later. Ug'd allas miss school the next day or three and when he came back he showed signs of the promised whippin'. I'll say I got mighty tired of that.

Tireder more even than I'd got of Buford allas trying to start a fracas, that was a word daddy'd used once and I liked the sound of it, allas trying to get my dander up. Once in a while, I'd have at him. Buford wasn't getting any smaller, but I was getting bigger. Momma said I outgrew the clothes she let out for me before she was done with the lettin' out!

I was tired of Pus Ug's daddy, so one day I asked my daddy about it. "Why do we let Daddy Ug beat up on Pus, when we oughtn't do it ourselves or let the kids at the schoolhouse do it neither?"

"Well, boy, a man's son is his own business. I wouldn't want Mister Ug down here telling me what's what with the raising of my own little ones. I don't reckon you would either." He was right as rain about that! I didn't want Pus Ug's daddy anywhere near me, truth being told. He was whip-thin and wore a hangy-down mustache that was allas crusted up with food or sick or snot. When he grabbed Ug and took him home, the muscles under his skin looked like a bag of snakes, all wriggling and fighting to get free. My daddy would catch snakes and put 'em in a bag to let loose in our garden. They ate up the mice and rats and bugs, he said.

Came a day sissa got the chickenpox. I never did know why they called them the chickenpox, until I seen sissa. She looked like she'd got pecked all over by some terrible angry rooster! Well, Momma and Daddy'd both never had the chickenpox, and the Doc said how they should keep clear for want of having 'em before. He told us we ought think about getting 'em, so we'd be safe later. I didn't want chickenpox, though. Brother was too scared to get 'em.

That left no one but the Doc to take care of little sissa, and he had other calls on his attention. He couldn't be always at our place. Then Pus Ug heard about the chickenpox, and right off he says, 'I've had them things.' Then he come home with me and took care of sissa. Stayed up with her nights and played games with her to keep her occupied and stop her itching them pox.

Wiped her down with a cool cloth and then boiled all the bedclothes himself when she wasn't con-tay-jus no more, so none of us had to get sick.

Sissa was the best part of mended when Pus Ug's daddy came on down Briar Creek Road looking for him.

"Where's my boy at, Maclellan?" Pus' daddy shouted. He allas shouted, never a quiet word from Mister Ug. "I know he's around here, damn it. Them damn hogs need lookin' after!"

I knew from the jump something was different, cause Daddy went walking right out to see Mister Ug. He hadn't never done that before. "That boy'll be staying on here the year, Silas." That was Pus' daddy's name, I guessed. "You go on home and see to them hogs yourself."

Mister Silas Ug's snaky old arms got all bunched up and he squared his head down 'tween his shoulders, like a bull ready to make a run. "You'll want to bring my boy out here directly, Maclellan, or I'll give you a taste of what he's got in store." My daddy just stood there with his arms folded over his chest, like they was talkin' about the weather. Mister Ug pulled back one of his arms real slow, showin' us all he was gonna throw the biggest haymaker we ever did see and still my daddy din't do nothin'!

Then Mister Silas Ug swung that haymaker and knocked my daddy down. Us kids was in the dooryard, feeding the chickens. Momma was back in the house, and she hollered out, "James! Stay down!" Everyone out there could hear her thumb back the hammer on daddy's Winchester rifle. "You get home, Silas Ug. You get home and you don't ever come back here again!"

I guess that's what my folks meant about the Scots having a whole lot of fight in 'em. Silas Ug did go, and he left his farm behind too since he was so embarrassed to be drove off by a woman. Daddy took it over, and cared for them hogs right alongside Pus. That was how Pus came to stay with us.

Sometimes he'd still be like he was with his daddy. One time he accidentally let all the hogs loose. Pus just started cryin' and cryin'. So I asked him, "What are you cryin' for ninny?"

Daddy was there with us, and he told me, "Don't call your brother a ninny, Charlie." I figured Pus was my brother ever since he took care of sissa. He was a better brother than Brother! "C'mon Pus, we better round up them hogs." Daddy said. Pus was still cryin' though.

"Just do it! I know you want to! Just get it over with!" Pus screamed at Daddy.

Daddy took his shoulder, even though Pus flinched away. "Do what, son?"

"Go on and beat me! I'm a dunce and no good and deserve it, so just do it!" Pus was all out of breath from cryin' so hard and had to yell between big gulps of air.

Daddy looked puzzled at him and said, "Am I just supposed to forget that I love you, Pus?" Pus needs reminding of that every so often. That's how Pus Ug, a neighbor on Briar Creek Road, got to be my brother.

An essay by Charlie Maclellan

TRUTH SEEKERS LLC

Sascha rolled her chair away from the desk and stretched luxuriantly. She had been data mining for hours, and deserved a break. Across the lab, James watched appreciatively.

Sascha raised an eyebrow. "Something?"

"Just enjoying the show. Find anything else?" James was poring over actual books spread out on the triangle of tables he surrounded himself with while he worked. He kept saying that there was information that couldn't be found on the Internet.

Sascha had to admit, he was right. Occasionally. "Just confirming what we already know. It never hurts to double check. Or in this case, quadruple check. You?"

"I've found a new name or two as owners of that island going all the back to the French colonists, it seems. There's even a missionary account or two saying that the island tribes held the place in deep superstitious dread." The information James dug up was always less immediately relevant to the case they were working, but it came in handy at the oddest of moments.

"Hmph. We'd already be on this case if Chu would show up. When was his last report? Months ago?" The two of them had worn this conversation down to nothing through repetition, but Sascha couldn't help herself. Chu was the field agent to their lab geekiness. He was working a case in Massachusetts, and had been for nearly a year.

"Look, he's probably stuck cataloging the whole damn place. You saw the square footage, who knows how many dusty old crates were jammed in there?" James knew as well as Sascha that Chu had gone far too long without sending a report. The place he was investigating was an old warehouse, built in the back of beyond in 1856. It was a miracle the place was still standing at all. Stand it did though, and, according to the research, it contained the contents of the cabinets of curiosity from the City of New York. The cabinets not bought out by the Museum of Natural History, anyway.

Cabinets of curiosity were the progenitors of modern curio cabinets and museums, and like dinosaurs to modern turtles, they had been enormous and varied. The word cabinet itself once meant a room, and 1600-1800s collectors of curiosities had filled rooms with strange, wonderful items. Natural phenomena, automata, medical oddities, sculpture, paintings, anything that could inspire wonder. The old cabinets were eventually concentrated, monetized, and maintained by professional curators, becoming museums. Some had slipped through the cracks though, and it seemed that most of those that had, had ended up in that old Massachusetts warehouse.

The research had taken months. The plot of land the building sat on had gone through nearly as many owners as years it had been standing. The contents' ownership was an even more entangled issue, if that was possible. The rumor was that buried somewhere in the massive collection was a mummified skunk-ape. Pulled from a peat bog outside New York, went the story, when the whites were draining them all to put up buildings. Unique skeletal structure, musculature still intact, incredibly well preserved. Of course, the sole account was from an ancient newspaper James managed to find. Still, it was the sort of thing their team did, for the right price.

The team was an odd group. James Frogge hailed from

Maine, and when asked where, he would state 'Innsmouth' and give a wide smile. He even wore his Innsmouth swim team shirt, on occasion. Sascha Tesla had come to the United States illegally, originally brought over as part of the lucrative white slave trade. In a month, she was running the books for the illicit operation. In six months, she turned over every facet of the business to the FBI. Her name hadn't been Sascha Tesla then. The last member of the team was Chin Shoo Chu. He was born in Iowa and raised there among the corn fields, fifth generation American. He was the most normal person either of the other two knew. He had a way with people, a sunny, friendly disposition and he loved investigating.

That was their business, investigating. Or digging. Some people called it not leaving well enough alone. They specialized in the weird. Chu started the business after he graduated college and gotten licensed as a private detective everywhere there were licenses. He had always been fascinated by the strange, the unexplained and the mysterious. The team had a bad rap among fraudsters as debunkers, but they really were believers. First and foremost, in the truth. That was the company name, after all: Truth Seekers, LLC.

Their funding came from sources as strange as the jobs they acquired. Sometimes private, sometimes governmental, sometimes even foreign, like the case James and Sascha were currently working. The government of Cuba, recently experiencing an influx of capital due to reopening its borders, was looking to get some positive publicity by getting its nation in the news. What better way than talking up some of the more exotic myths about the little islands Cuba lay claim to? It was only one of the many ways its new tourism industry was trying to get on the map, but Truth Seekers was glad for the income.

"I know the place was huge, and probably filled with dried monkey heads, bottled two-headed snakes and ancient, worthless family heirlooms. Still, the guy could send an e-mail." Sascha was just bending back over her keyboard when they heard the outer door of the lab open.

"Expecting someone?" James asked.

"No. You?" Sascha was already reaching for the Walther PPK she kept in her bottom desk drawer. They weren't the type of place to get robbed. At least, they hadn't been until they investigated the wreck of an ancient Spanish galleon off the coast of the Yucatan and found enough doubloons to drown in. It was amazing how many idiots thought that 1.) the treasure was on the premises and 2.) that Truth Seekers got to keep anything meaningful out of it. The company had been instrumental in determining the date of the storm that wrecked the ship, when the ship set out, and what the most likely location of the wreck was in a five mile radius. The company had not received a heap of gold for its trouble.

"No." James was frowning, and with a mouth as wide as his it was one impressive frown. He was already fiddling underneath one of his tables. He kept a sawed-off shotgun strapped there for the same reason Sascha kept her PPK. They heard steps coming slow, sounding like whoever was walking in was dragging one foot. Sascha checked her safety, James broke open his double barreled and calmly inserted two shells he had produced from somewhere. He nodded over to her.

The door to the research room opened, and the fluorescent light from the hall flooded into the dim environment, temporarily blinding the two armed researchers. The figure in the door was wearing a long, dark overcoat.

"You're not going to shoot me, are you?" Chu asked, and he looked awful.

Sascha and James made Chu as comfortable as possible before he started to talk about the year he'd been away. Even after a cup of hot tea and a thick blanket, Chu still looked awful. His eyes were sunken, his skin had a waxy look, and he was pale as the winter moon. When he walked in, he displayed a heavy limp in his right leg. He looked ten years older than he did when he left.

"What you have to understand," he began, "is that I've been gone longer than a year."

Sascha quirked an eyebrow. "Is this where you tell us you've been cheating with another discovery firm?"

James kept frowning.

"No. Not quite." Chu answered with his trademark half-smile. "What I found—what we found is going to change everything."

"Is it bigger than the galleon?" James put in.

"Bigger."

Sascha stood up. "I'll pack. You can tell us about it on the way."

The warehouse stood alongside Horlicks University in the oldest part of Lichberg, Massachusetts. Of course, it hadn't been a warehouse for all its long existence. The building had been a theater, dance hall, car dealership, armory and various other functions. It was built in the old armory fashion, all weathered brick and crumbling mortar now, but still standing. When it was converted into a warehouse, the armory's front doors were widened out to accommodate wagons and later, trucks that would drop their shipments where ever there was room in the haphazardly arranged interior. Exterior sliding doors were installed to make more space in the building.

Chu stood in front of the old brick building, staring up at it. The masonry reached a height of four stories at the peak of the roof. He shook his head and commented over his shoulder. "Hard to believe this is only the fifth or sixth time I've been here, isn't it?"

Sascha was carefully rolling some equipment cases down their rented moving van's ramp. "Yes, considering you were out of touch for a year and we assumed you were here the whole time. You're going to have to go over that again. I'm still having trouble wrapping my head around it."

James held his cell phone up, searching for a signal. "Huh. One lousy bar. Wireless network of the future, my ass."

"It'll get worse, the closer we get." Chu was still staring at the building.

James put his phone away and narrowed his eyes at the nearby university grounds. "Horlicks. I thought about attending here, you know. Time was, they had an excellent biology program. History department has always been dreadful, though. Sascha, let me help you with some of that."

Sascha was shouldering her laptop bag and pushing the ramp back into its storage compartment. "Nice timing, Frogge. Just for that, I'm making you run all the network connections and power cables."

Chu listened to his partners' banter with half an ear. Most of his mind was far away, as lost as he had been for ten long years in the discovery of a lifetime.

"The best way I can describe it is by calling it a mirror." Chu began. "But, it isn't really a mirror. No reflections are visible in it, not even light. Bringing a light closer to it has all the effect of bringing a light closer to a tree. It simply becomes more visible. The surface is polished to a mirror sheen, however, and the cabinet that was built around it was Victorian-era woodwork." He paused a moment to think.

Sascha was driving the moving van. "So it looks like a mirror, but doesn't act like a mirror, and you found it in a cabinet. Wait, that's not what you said."

Chu smiled. He'd missed Sascha. "No, it's not. The cabinet

had to be built around it because it isn't a mirror. Whatever it is, it can't be moved."

James, who normally spent long car rides with his head buried in a book, was rapt. "It's too fragile?" he asked.

"No. Quite the opposite. I tried to bring the cabinet out of the building, and could not move it. Eventually, I disassembled the entire thing. What was left looked even less like a mirror than it did before. Breaking down the cabinetry revealed something else as well." Chu stopped, not sure how much to say. He had to keep reminding himself he was home now, and back with his team. There was a time he would have automatically trusted these two, his closest friends. That time wasn't so long ago, to them.

"Well? What did it look like, Chu? Was it bigger than a breadbox?" Sascha asked.

"By quite a lot. It appeared to be a crystal, cut flat or ground flat on the bottom, though I was still unable to shift it an inch. When I say crystal, you may be picturing a hand span of quartz, or a shiny piece of gypsy flummery. What I'm talking about looked like it came from Naica."

James shifted in his seat. "The Cave of Swords wasn't discovered in Naica until 1910, and the really large deposits not until 2000. How big are we talking?" Naica, Mexico had been the home of a mine since silver was first discovered there in the turn of the 20th. Mining continued when significant deposits of lead and zinc were found.

"This piece could have come from the 2000 find. The size, and the authenticity of the cabinetry I took apart, means that the thing could not have come from the only known place it could have naturally formed."

"Now we're getting somewhere." Sascha mumbled. It was hard to know if she meant about the find or about passing an old couple in a Cadillac.

"I was unable to scratch, chip or flake it to run tests on a sample. I call it a crystal because that's what it looks like, but I couldn't verify that assumption."

"Further down the rabbit hole. A big chunk of material that appears to be a crystal and interacts strangely with human vision. If it is a natural crystal, it must have formed in an unknown place. If it was artificially grown, it was done with technology that was unknown at the time the cabinet was built around it. Go on." Sascha had a knack for summing up.

"Ah—Alright. So there was one there one other thing I found when I took apart the cabinet." Chu grabbed a messenger bag from the floor of the vehicle, between his feet. He carefully removed an antique-looking paper envelope from it and handed it wordlessly to James.

"Without running any tests, my analysis is that this," James said as he examined the paper and the single word written on it, "is very old. This says 'Control'. Control what? And how?"

"Those questions are better answered by demonstration, I think." Chu took the envelope back and stored it carefully. "Here's what was in it." He reached into his inner jacket pocket and brought out a quarter circle of dull, gray metal. It was flat, almost impossibly thin. He fiddled for a moment and it ... opened. The quarter circle became an arc, and then a full circle. The thickness of the metal never seemed to change, and there were no visible hinges. When it was fully unfolded, the circle was large enough for a grown man to put his arm through. Which Chu promptly did, up to his shoulder.

"What the f—" Sascha began to exclaim, but Chu cut her off with a hiss.

"Quiet! This takes concentration!" Chu had put his arm through the circle, but it didn't come out the other side. His arm just ... ended at the shoulder. His face was drawn in a rictus of effort as he did whatever he did wherever his arm went.

Suddenly, he yanked his arm out, and with it came a telescoping tube, made from the same gray metal as the circle. It floated impossibly in the center of the circle, while Chu counted levels of the metal. "Eight, nine, ten. Hm. I thought I'd get the full thirteen."

"Chu, what the hell is going on here? What is that thing?" James asked from the back seat.

"This? This is just the beginning, my friends."

Sascha edged the moving van's speed up.

The computers were up and the trio moved silently around the object Chu had covered with a sheet. James and Sascha stealing glances from the corners of their eyes, Chu ignoring it.

"My wi-fi isn't working." Sascha complained.

"It won't. We'll have to find hard line for you to use. Once we activate it," Chu waved vaguely at the sheet, "all the telecoms will stop working. I've got a beta site set up in an empty lab at the university where the equipment will work fine."

Sascha nudged James. "Hard line, Frogge. You got cable duty, remember?"

"Yeah. I'm on it. This place is amazing, Chu. You barely got through a quarter of the collections." James said as he wandered into the dusty, stacked crates.

"I think what we'll do here will put your mind at ease, James." Chu called after him. He turned back to find Sascha with her hand out.

"Give me the ringy-thingy."

Chu slowly shook his head. "Nope. You have no idea how dangerous the control can be. I barely got away with my life the first time I futzed with it."

"You're kidding. I need to start analyzing it right away. That piece alone will make our names forever." Sascha's eastern European accent was creeping back into her voice, a sign that Chu was being disappointing to his tech witch.

"I'm not kidding Sascha. We are going to analyze this thing, and figure it out. We're going to do it together, with all three of us involved in each step. What we're not going to do is make the kind of mistake that sent me away for ten years." Chu stopped suddenly, realizing he had possibly said too much.

"Ten years? Chu, what the hell is this thing?"

"You'll see. You'll both see."

Chu whipped the sheet off the mirror. It stood a few inches taller than six feet and was three feet at its thickest point, across the base. It was polished to a high sheen, though if what Chu said was true about being unable to affect the material, the effect must have been natural. What Chu said about the visual peculiarities was very true; the mirror held no reflections. Both James and Sacha, true to their sense of professionalism, gawked for only a few minutes before they scrambled for instruments to start measuring the mirror. The team brought spectrometers, audio and video recorders, a portable chemistry lab, Geiger-Müller counters and various other implements to not only take the physical dimensions of the item, but also measure every known emission the mirror might create. James, ever the technological Luddite whenever possible, was setting up an antique General Electric alternating current ammeter, wiring leads to more modern medical sensor pads. They wouldn't stick to the surface of the mirror.

"Damn. This mirror of yours really resists any kind of being interfered with, Chu." James was measuring out a length of nonreactive string to tie the leads onto the object.

"Our mirror, James." Chu gently corrected him. "Believe me, you haven't seen anything yet. You may not want to attach those sensors anyway. The mirror reacts strongly to the control."

"Strongly?" Sascha asked. "How far away should we be setting up?"

"Honestly, I have no idea. Are we ready to record and take readings?" Chu gently, gently took the control out of his pocket and laid it on one of the tables they had set up.

"Ready." James replied.

"Green." Sascha said.

"Ok. Let's talk about what happened the last time I did this, so you'll know what to expect."

"It took me weeks at the beta site to figure out how to unfold the control after I found it. There were no instructions, and there are no visible seams or buttons. The way has to be felt, rather than seen. Once I had made it into the full circle, I never thought to reach into the hoop. Until I was cataloging the cabinet parts, and dropped my pen into it." Chu stared at the thin metal quarter circle that lay on the table.

"What happened?" Sascha asked in a tiny voice.

"Not quite what I expected. The pen was just sitting on the table, but when I reached for it... When I reached for it I grabbed the pen, but my hand just disappeared for a second into the tabletop. It felt not unlike accidentally touching a live contact in a fuse box. There was a strange, bone deep vibration, but any heat created was immediately leeched away. It was cold." Chu tore his eyes away from the thing to look at his two friends. They were rapt, having seen the control in action, they waited for what came next. Chu sighed.

"How long did you wait before reaching in purposefully?" James's voice was next door to a whisper.

"An hour. Maybe two. It seems so long ago, now. Huh. It

was so long ago." Chu sank into one of the folding chairs they had set up. "You both saw the telescoped metal I pulled out of the ring. Back in the car, I counted off ten layers. There are a total of thirteen. When I use the control in conjunction in the mirror, an image appears there. Depending on which layer is the last showing on the control, a different image appears."

"So, not a mirror. A window then?" James leaned back with his arms crossed, his subtly too-wide eyes fixed on the mirror.

"Not exactly. It took me a while, but I learned that a twist of the telescope on the control can have an effect as well. The control can change the mirror into a window, and then into a doorway." Chu looked at his hands, turning them over and over, as if they were new.

"A doorway to where?" Sascha asked.

"Not quite the right question."

"What do you mean?" she said.

"Try a different 'w'."

"When?" James said.

"When." Chu confirmed.

"A doorway into time..." Sascha said in wonder.

"Better to say through time, with specific points into which it could open. Thirteen, to be exact." Chu was still looking at his hands, speaking softly. "Thirteen possibilities. Which do you suppose I stepped into, when I did? When did I end up?"

James uncrossed his arms and stared at the mirror with new respect. "The thirteenth. Most likely the furthest away in terms of time, and, from what you've told us, the most difficult to access."

"Lucky thirteen." Chu said. "Lucky. Let's put the sheet back over that thing and order something to eat. This may take longer than I thought."

One of the folding tables was festooned with city blocks of containers from a Chinese carry-out. James clicked his chopsticks as he reached for another crab rangoon, and Chu spun his fork in a paper bowl of lo mein. Sascha picked at a plate of potstickers.

"You said it was a doorway. So you stepped through?" She pushed some cabbage around the edge of her plate.

"I did," Chu said around a mouthful of noodles. "But let me finish eating."

Sascha loaded her fork with vegetables and catapulted the contents at Chu. "This is all old news to you, Chu, but you owe us an explanation. Talk!"

James put his rangoon in his mouth, whole, and crunched down. "Yeah, Chu. Don't keep us in suspense."

Chu set his fork down and laid his hands on the table on either side of his bowl. "Alright. But don't be surprised if you lose your appetite. You were right, I had to go to the furthest era I could reach. When I manipulated the control and pulled the telescope all the way out, the image that appeared showed this warehouse, only in burnt ruins. The mirror itself was partially obstructed by some fallen debris. Of course, I took precautions and tried a remote device at first. The passage through the doorway fried it. Only when I tried inert objects did they come back unscathed." He motioned to a push broom standing forgotten against some nearby crates. Soot was still caked around the bristles at the bottom. "I used that to clear the other side of the mirror before I went through. I'm saying that I took all the precautions, but believe me, I was wild to see what was on the other side. I took no time to contact you two, to measure any radiant energy from the mirror, nothing. I was obsessed with finally finding the exact world-changing thing that our entire careers have been about." He paused for a breath. It wasn't easy admitting that he had cut out his partners, who had been with him through the hard times and the good. "I stepped through as soon as the other side of the mirror was clear."

Sascha blew air out of her nose, annoyed. James sat and waited, with his strange, nearly inhuman calm.

"I had no way of knowing how long the mirror would be open after I stepped through, so I took the control with me. On the other side, it immediately reverted to its original, quarter circle shape. The mirror went dark at some point, but the time I spent goggling around prevented me from seeing how long it took. All around me, the warehouse was in cinders. The brick walls were tumbled down and heavily scorched. Almost nothing remained of the crates and collections that surround us now, and there was something else. The campus grounds, the quad, the boulevard, everything was black and dead. The only thing moving was the wind." The memory pressed close on Chu, making him see it all again, even though it had been ten years since that first time he stepped through the mirror to find the blasted future beyond.

"Nuclear? Atomic?" Sascha murmured.

"Meteor? Volcano?" James grumbled.

"War." Chu said. "The last war, I assume. Beyond the mirror, the world had changed irrevocably. You have to understand that man no longer fought against man in a struggle to accumulate wealth or righteousness or land. Man struggled to survive and find his place in a world where he had been displaced as the dominant life form on Earth."

"Aliens. Or singularity." Sascha said definitively.

"Disease. Vengeful, ancient gods." James rattled off without blinking. The team did specialize in the weird.

"Evolution, or all of the above." Chu agreed. "You see, the first living thing I came across on the far side of the mirror was a weeping willow tree. I had no idea what kind of danger I was in. The thing stood thirty feet tall at its crown. Its long, waving branches were stained by what I assumed to be soot and ash. The greenery drew me on like a magnet. There is something in the human soul that draws us towards nature, towards green, growing things. So I went to the willow, telling myself I wanted to examine it. The truth is, in that world of blackened buildings, cracked asphalt and rotting automobiles, I just wanted something familiar to touch." Chu held his hands up, showing his partners the silvery, smooth scars across their backs.

"The willow must have felt the same about me, because it reached out. It reached out, and it nearly took me. At first I thought the branches were stirring in the breeze. Then I realized there was no more breeze. Then it had me. I had subconsciously reached out to the thing, and the long, hanging fronds reached back. It wrapped my hands in a blur of green motion and tightened like a constrictor. Pulsing beneath the thin, smooth bark I could see an orange luminescence. I yanked my hands back like I had touched a hot stove, but it was too late. The willow had me fast. It began to drag me forward." He traced each thin line with the opposite hand.

"How did you get away?" Sascha had stopped eating her pot stickers.

"I lowered my head and bit through the branches, of course. More of the branches whipped at my scalp." Chu spread his thick hair, showing more scars on his head. "But I got away. When I bit through the wood, that orange light made more sense. The sap had become bio luminescent, I assume for the same reasons that fireflies or squid evolved the feature. I could see the orange light coming off my face as I backed away, holding my hands to my chest to staunch the bleeding. The taste was indescribably bitter. I retreated to the mirror, which I noted had not a single smudge of the omnipresent soot on its surface, and tried the control. My blood and the pain made the process of unfolding the circle difficult. When I reached through the control, my arm just went through. It didn't react like it had before. Then I heard a rustling, the sound of a tree in the wind.

The willow was pulling up its roots, the orange light beneath its bark pulsing faster than ever. It was coming after me. I had no choice but to run."

"Run where? Where did you go?" James asked.

"Anywhere. Nowhere. It didn't matter, as long as I was somewhere without grass, without trees and with a healthy fire going. I understood why the world was scorched, but not why the control had stopped working. I needed to figure it out." Chu looked back to the control, his eyes unreadable. "I headed across the ruined campus towards the shell of the library. That was where I found the first living people."

"Living? There were corpses?" Sascha pushed her plate away and leaned back from table.

"I didn't recognize them at first. Burnt, twisted up into the fetal position from the heat of the fires, I came to know the sight very well. Some had been devoured by the orangelight plant life."

James had pulled out a notepad from somewhere. "Orangelight plants? Were there others?"

"I found out that not all plants had awakened and not all had that strange orange bio luminescence. Those that did though, those were the dangerous ones. Trees especially so."

"You found out? These people told you, then?" Sascha asked.

"Yes. You have to understand, these people looked at me the same way we would look at a medieval knight who just stepped out of history. I was clothed in mainly plant fibers, cotton to be exact, along with rubber-soled shoes. Most of the cotton had gone orangelight a decade before my arrival, making wearing it akin to wearing wolf skins. After the kelp turned, shipments of the necessary products to make artificial rubber stopped completely. These people were wearing—" Chu stopped, searching for the right words. "They were wearing the clothing and shoes made from the only common material."

"The human body." James said as he jotted notes. "It follows that if the plant life became unusable. Our herbivore products would be mostly gone, along with the plant fiber products."

Chu nodded. "Yes. Clothing woven from human hair, shoes from tanned leather."

"They hunted each other instead of the plants?" Sascha put in, fascinated and disgusted all at once.

"No. They simply made use of their dead. After they take the usable parts, they leave the rest far from their camp to keep the scavenger bluelights away. There's a whole new ecosystem there, and it's still shaking itself out." Chu collected himself.

"Ten years, Chu. How did you get stuck there ten years?" Sascha was staring at the control with a mingled look of dread and eagerness.

"At first it was because I couldn't get back to the mirror. I spent a year trying."

"What about the control? Did you get it working again?" James asked.

"Yes. It was a simple mistake. I had tried to use it the wrong way 'round. I was on the other side of the mirror, you see?" Chu barked a laugh that didn't sound exactly humorous. "I didn't know it, but the university grounds were a favorite hunting ground for the orangelights. There was always an oak or a pack of spruce prowling around. It was too dangerous. Too dangerous, and—you two didn't see these people. They needed help, they needed leadership. At least, that's what I told myself."

"You needed to find out what happened." Frogge said flatly.

"To see if you could prevent it here." Sascha added hopefully.

"We call ourselves Truth Seekers, after all." Chu sighed. "Yes, I needed to find out what had happened and if it was preventable. Those people really did need my help, though. If you could have seen how they were, you would agree with me. That year I spent trying to get back to the mirror was also spent observing and cataloging the new floral order. The old decorative plants, hostas, roses, juniper, trumpet vines, gladiolas, and so on were nearly wiped out due to over predation. They were some of the few plants left that were content still to be plants. They developed a green bio luminosity. It made them targets for not only the hungry humans and what little livestock remained, but also the other plant life. The greenlights were easy prey for everything that moved, just like the older order of vegetation had been." Chu looked around the big warehouse, pulling himself out of his memories.

"Are you O.K.? Do you want to stop?" James asked, pen still poised over paper.

"Yes. No. I need to get through this, for your sakes. And for my own, I suppose. I led those people away from the dangerous university grounds and towards what I remembered as being the suburbs of Lichberg. That was going to be the most likely place to find the greenlights we would need to start rebuilding. Greenlights, and I hoped for lawn care equipment." Chu said with a wolfish grin. "These people were equipped with spears made from lashed-together leg bones and clubs from femurs. Steel would go a long way toward evening up the odds with things like that orangelight willow that gave me these scars. It took a another year to scavenge the outskirts fully. We gathered seeds, steel and most importantly of all, confidence. The first time we took down an evergreen was a good day. It showed the survivors that the orangelights could be brought down. The things were barely animal intelligence, after all. Men have ever been the masters of beasts. Roasted pine nuts never tasted so good."

Sascha fidgeted, plainly wanting to begin, but also hanging on each word from Chu. "That's two years spent beyond the mirror. What did you do for the other eight?"

"I led. I led them into the farmlands, and taught them how to build, how to write and read, and how to fight. That most of all. I had found my answer while I was digging through suburbs, you see, and I had to get back. To get back, I would need to come in force to the university grounds and hold them long enough to get through the mirror. To get back, I would need an army. So I trained one." Chu reached into the messenger bag he had brought from the truck. He carefully brought out a folded scrap of newspaper, yellowed with age and blackened around the edges. There was no date, and the text was incomplete. "There isn't enough here to be able to tell when this all happened, but according to this, it was an experiment in building a more pest resistant crop. I guess they didn't count on the crops deciding that humans were the biggest pests of all. The 'lightquake' as they call it here was spread unstoppably by the forces of wind, rain, and insect pollination." Chu took a breath.

James grunted. "Argh."

"Bees." Sascha agreed.

Chu smiled. "It was a wonder, at first. Plants that could seek out water sources, plants that could cross pollinate to create newer, stronger strains. They were all greenlights, at first. It didn't take long for that to change, according to the stories my survivors told. The bluelights were the first variants, followed by the redlights. The redlights were even worse than the orange, apparently. The redlights were the reason men scorched the earth. The orangelights were opportunists, like bears. The red, well the red were more like sharks. Perfect killing and eating machines. The war lasted until the supply chains broke down. What was left were just pockets of humanity, scratching out a pathetic shadow of life in the twilight of their great dominance."

"Did you ever see one of the redlights?" James asked, ever the cataloger.

Chu looked wan. "Once. The day we assaulted the

university. My entrance had woken something up. It took years for the thing to free itself up from the deep roots it had sunk, but it was there, squatting over the warehouse site like it knew. Like it knew, and was waiting for me."

"What was it?" Sascha asked in a near whisper.

"A Populus grandidenta." Chu used the Latin name.

Frogge automatically translated. "A Bigtooth Aspen."

"A Bigtooth Aspen." Chu confirmed. "The Aspen tree survives forest fires, since most of the tree is made of a complex root system. It only sends shoots above ground."

"Right. The Utah Aspen colony, Pando, is supposed to be 80,000 years old." Sascha had her laptop out and was punching up information as automatically as James had translated the Latin name.

"The thing had set itself up on the site of the warehouse. The mirror was stuck in the middle of a grove of redlight Bigtooth Aspen. We had the training, the weapons and the people. God help me, I sent them in there." Chu raised a shaking hand to his brow. "I sent them in there knowing not one in three would come out again. While they fought and died, I went for the mirror. I rationalized it, you see?"

Frogge set his pen gently down next to the pad he had been writing on. "If you got back here, you could keep any of it from ever happening. You could stop the lightquake before it ever got started."

"I'm back. They died to get me here, but I'm back. We have to figure out where this thing starts and how to stop it. I think our best shot at it lies in figuring out how the mirror works. If we can manipulate that, we can go somewhen else on the time line and get better information." Chu lowered his hand. "We have to stop it."

Sascha looked up from her laptop, her face hard in its soft glow. "We will."

The equipment was ready, and the recording instruments both on site and at the beta site were functioning properly. It was time to activate the control.

"At first, I'm just going to activate the mirror. We can get some readings, analyze the data and then figure out what our next step is." Chu warned his team again. Truth be told, they probably didn't need the warning. However, they could both tell Chu was terrified of something going wrong and getting stuck in the mirror again. He was telling himself as much as he was telling them. James and Sascha let him have his say. "Clear?"

Tesla checked her laptop's master control readout. "Ready on my end, Chu."

James made a last check mark on a list he had clipped to a clipboard and nodded. "Video and audio are go, Chu. Whenever you're ready."

Chu took a deep breath and unfolded the control.

Sascha raised an eyebrow behind her screen as several energy readings immediately jumped into the abnormal range. "Getting some radiant energy, across several spectra. Nothing too wild yet, but definitely higher amounts than normal background."

Chu nodded to her, sweat obvious on his brow. He spoke mostly under his breath, "Here goes, you bastard." He shoved his arm into the circle and grimaced with the discomfort. His face settled into a determined scowl as he groped in the impossible space created within the ring of the control and then slowly he began to draw the telescope out. James was writing furiously without looking away, committing his memories to a non-electronic form in case the equipment failed. As Chu drew the telescope slowly out, images began to flicker past in the mirror. Fragmentary, momentary glimpses into possible reflections, like the memory of a memory from a dream. The tendons in Chu's neck were standing out, looking like steel cables. He applied, steady smooth strength, drawing the telescope out level by level until he had all thirteen exposed. There was still a small gap between the edge of the thirteenth level and the edge of the control.

"Holy Mother of God," Tesla whispered, "the Bigtooth." Beyond the mirror, there was what should have been an idyllic forest scene. White aspen trunks stood proud, and the golden leaves carpeted the ground below. Low hanging branches were draped with the beautiful leaves as well. It should have been idyllic, but it wasn't. Like veins crawling up a skinless arm, red lines pulsed all along the branches and throughout the leaves. It looked like nothing less than a nervous system torn out and laid open to the air. The Bigtooth was reacting to the energy emitted from the mirror, and the visible branches began to thrash.

Chu tried very hard not to look at the irregular, human sized lumps scattered about on the other side of mirror, covered by a layer of leaves.

Sascha tore her eyes away from the mirror and looked to her control suite. "It's getting weird." she murmured.

"It's trying to come through." James said with a calm that was somehow more shocking than if he had screamed it. "Chu, close down the control." The redlit tips of the white branches were already coming through. "Chu. Please terminate the connection." Chu was frozen in horror, staring at the thing through the mirror.

"Chu! Shut it down!" Tesla screamed from behind her screen. The massive energy outputs were creeping into the danger zone for her equipment, which meant that human exposure was about to become fatal. "Now!" Chu flinched heavily, recoiling from the mirror and pushing hard against the telescope protruding from the control. The Bigtooth had six feet of itself through the mirror already, and the branch was scratching about on the concrete floor with a soft scraping sound, searching for something to grab onto and heave more of its bulk through. Chu got the thirteenth level of the telescope through the control and mirror resumed its former opacity as he pushed the rest of the telescope rapidly through and whipped his arm back before the control could fold itself back up. James and Sascha were staring at something behind him. He turned slowly and looked.

Just six inches short of his feet the end of the Bigtooth branch lay twitching. Its far end spread glowing red smears on the floor at the bottom of the mirror, but the fluid seemed to simply run from the sloped surface of the mirror itself. Chu spoke harshly, his voice sounding ragged. "Get the hazmat suit. We burn it in situ after erecting an air tight seal around it. Charcoal filter the smoke, seal the filters and the ashes in biohazard bags and then put the whole works in a safe that we forget the combination to and bury in cement. None of this," he said as he gestured to the branch, "comes into contact with any flora from our side. We cannot risk contamination." James and Sascha nodded silently. "Let's go."

The branch was disposed of safely and the team agreed to retire for the evening. They each went to their rooms in the nearby hotel for an hour or so. Chu made it the longest, and he found the other two already at work at the beta site when he got there.

"You guys too, huh?" he asked his partners. They each smiled at him as he walked into the lab.

Sascha waved him over. "This find is too big. Too important. Have a look at this." She had brought up the energy readings from the experiment. Chu stared at the screen. He had been away for ten years, she hadn't.

"What am I looking at?" he asked.

"On a whim, I monitored everything coming off the mirror, including radio waves." Sascha explained.

"Radio transmissions?" Chu was staring at the spiky

readouts. They clearly denoted activity.

"Sort of. At any rate, I found something. It's weak as hell, but I think I can refine it." Sascha was already fiddling with another program as she talked to Chu. James was waving him over to the familiar triangle of tables the man preferred to work in.

"Good. Let me know when you make more progress." Chu said as he walked away. "James?"

"Hey Chu. I've been examining the scrap of newspaper you brought back. It's... Well it's interesting." James looked up from his work, a loupe over one eye magnifying the strangeness of his wide face.

"How so?" Chu asked as he leaned over the table to get a look through the microscope set up there.

"It's the ink. It's a cephalopod byproduct. Octopus or squid ink, in other words." James waited for Chu to be surprised.

"And?" Chu asked.

"That's what I said at first, too. Since most ink is made with soy, and the flora up and rebelled I'm sure they had to find another source of ink. Only—" James pushed his loupe back onto his head as Chu finished for him.

"Only this article is from before things got really bad. They'd still have had vats of the stuff." Chu frowned.

"Right. It gets weirder. Here in the States, we never used cephalopod ink to print newspaper. First it was a simple charcoal suspension, then petroleum based, and finally mostly soy based." James shrugged. "Like I said, interesting."

Chu was working out some implications when his gut went cold. "Sascha! Forget refining the source of that signal for second. Can you give me the audio?"

Sascha immediately began punching keys. "Coming up, though the interference is going to be nasty." The garbled transmission played, and hardly any of it was clear enough to understand.

"Welc... ympic G... aint Louis..." it said.

"When were the Olympic games held in Saint Louis?" Chu asked.

"1904." James rattled off. "The Olympic committee would never go back there after the coercion Saint Louis used to get the games in the first place. You see—" James was ready as ever to talk about people long dead and the feuds they had with each other, but Sascha cut him off.

"I just checked the sonic readouts. Call it a hunch that was going to be your next question, Chu. Answer mine first though: Did we bring a jackhammer?"

Chu shook his head. "No, but we can get one. And my next question, Sascha? It was going to be 'Where the Hell was I for ten years?'"

The control was tucked in Chu's jacket on the far side of the room. He looked over at it as Sascha braced to start hammering.

She scowled at the two men from behind her safety glasses before she started. "Tell me again why I'm doing this and you two are watching?"

"Your W.A.G., your hammer." Chu said stoically.

"W.A.G.?" she asked.

"Wild Ass Guess." James explained. "Now get to boun— hammering."

"Yeah, yeah. Apes." She checked her footing one last time before starting up the hammer. The noise was deafening in the enclosed space, and Chu was glad they had waited until morning to begin. Sascha chiseled straight lines into the concrete, creating a small grid. She kept going over the lines, getting deeper and deeper into the flooring until, suddenly, the jackhammer slipped out of her grip and disappeared down into the dark hole that had appeared inside her grid. "Oops. I was right."

"About what?" Chu asked.

"Remember how you told us about the cabinet being built around the mirror?" she said.

Chu leaned over the hole, careful to keep away from the weakened edges. "Yes. What are you saying?"

Sascha smiled and pushed her safety glasses up into her head. "That wasn't the only thing built around the mirror. The sonic readouts showed the floor was hollow here. This whole place was built around that thing."

"We'll need lights and rope."

James was already digging through the boxes to get the gear.

They tied the rope off around one of the roof support beams and slowly, carefully climbed down. The space below the floor wasn't a basement, it resembled more of a natural cave or hand dug root cellar. There was only one direction to follow once they were in and they set off down the damp, cramped corridor as carefully as possible.

"Who do you think dug this thing?" Sascha whispered.

"It could be natural. Is that?" James had trained his light on some painted figures on the rock wall. "Mi'kmaq rock art. Unbelievable! I've got to get a picture of this."

"Stay together!" Chu hissed at his team. "We have no idea what's down here, or what shape this cavern is in."

James looked abashed, but snapped his photo anyway. The small human figures were depicted as gathered around a large, spiky object, several times the size of any of them. One figure stood above the others, his arms over his head and a hoop in one hand. "Their medicine man. He's got the sacred hoop or circle of life in one hand, and—"

"Look, Frogge." Sascha held up her hand to cover the bottom of the object and most of the man holding the hoop. "What's that look like to you?" she asked.

"The mirror." he answered.

She nodded. "And that?"

"The control. How long has this thing been here?"

"Keep moving." Chu urged them along. There was more than just old paint on walls down there, he could feel it. They went another few yards and Sascha pointed her light upwards.

"Chu." she said, "What's that?"

He looked up to where she was pointing and saw immediately what she meant. It was wiring, and it was old. "Think it's still on the grid?" he asked her.

"It would explain some strange readings I got on the power draws for this place. This old wiring eats up amperage like nothing else." She followed the cables with her light down to a fixture. It had a bulb in it.

James examined it. "These old bulbs were almost immortal. I'll try switching it on." He pushed the switch and slowly, a yellow glow began to light up the corridor. "That's done it. Look, that must have been for the whole system." A faint yellow glow could be see further down the cavern.

"Huh." Chu grunted.

"What?" Sascha asked.

"Who switched it off?" Chu shivered a bit and told himself it was the cold, damp air. "Let's keep moving." Behind him, Sascha was still staring at the switch. James chivvied her forward. They moved further, and the floor took on a distinct downward slope. The cavern had been curving round to their right the entire time, hiding what was beyond more than a few yards from sight as they delved deeper.

Suddenly, where the tunnel would have been getting close to the mirror, the inner side of the curve opened up into a larger area. There were crystals, a huge formation, bigger than even Naica. They grew at every angle, forming a forest of non-reflective mirrors. Around each one was tied a simple knotted string with a paper envelope secured underneath it. Chu walked to the first one and stared at it. There was a single word written there. Without realizing it, he read it aloud.

"Control."

Drinks at the Sundown

It was a hot day in the middle of July the first and only time I served a drink to a dead man. Let me start earlier. I'm Jim Hauser, owner and operator of the Sundown Saloon. You can find me there most nights behind the bar and most days in my room above, puzzling out the ledger. It's not the easiest life, considering most of my patrons are liquored up and looking to fight, fuck or both. One never can say just who's going to be the next to step through those big bat-wing doors and just who's going to end pushing up daisies on Boot Hill. Even through all that beer, whiskey, blood and thunder, that day in the middle of July stands out to me.

The doors creaked in, like they always did. I reminded myself to grease those damn hinges, like I always did. The fella that walked in caught my attention right quick. He was bent over, like he'd been sneaking in to my joint (which isn't all that uncommon an occurrence) but he flinched away from everything, even those creaky old hinges. I know I don't keep the best bar on the frontier, but I defy you to find a pair of those damn doors that don't squeal like hogs at the trough. This fella though, this fella was putting his eyes all around the room, checking every angle of the floorboards and every shadow. I was standing at the bar with that damn ledger spread open in front of me, seeing as how my room upstairs had turned unbearable hot after noon.

He sidled up, still skittish like, and sat in the farthest stool from the door, with nothing but wall on his left side. He turned the stool so it faced the door. Once he was settled, (or as settled as I judged him like to get) I walked on down.

"Howdy, stranger. What can I pour for you?" I asked him, all smiles.

"There any other doors on this place?" he told me, which wasn't a drink at all.

"Yes sir, I've got a back door." I told him, which was normally a comfort to the folks that walked through my front door looking over their shoulders, like this fella had.

"Where." was all he said, all flat like that. Didn't even sound like a question, the way he said it. I just pointed. A barkeep is expected to take his lumps from the customers, but it was accepted that the bar would receive some custom prior to the lumps. "Anyone back there?" he went on, making an effort to ask half-ways nice.

"Yes, my cook is back there if you want some vittles. I'll do you a favor and warn you away from her porridge. Tastes about like sawdust, but stands thick as Georgia mud." I smiled as I said it, like I always did. I usually get a chuckle out of that one, if not many orders for porridge, but this fella wasn't the chuckling kind. Least ways, he didn't chuckle any.

The fella started to look a little more at his ease. "No, no, just a whiskey."

"Comin' right up." Now we were on more familiar territory for me. "Just ride into town?"

Most folks like a little conversation with a drink, but this fella just tossed back his whiskey and wiped his mouth with the back of one shaky hand. "Yeah. Another."

"And another. Let me welcome you to town then, stranger. It ain't much, but we call it home. Word is the railroad will be coming through here soon, if you're a stayer." I kept the bottle close. Any man could throw back the whiskey like that would need a steady pouring hand nearby. For his part, the fella turned white as a sheet.

"Why would you say that? What makes you mention the railroad?" He was really trying not to sound too demanding, but he sounded pretty demanding.

"Nothing much for big news around these parts mister. Rail coming through is about as big as a little town like this is going to get. Did I say something queer? You look like you seen a ghost." I said, which I thought was a common enough expression.

In response, the fella produced one of those navy revolvers and pointed it right at my chest. "Who the Hell are you!" he hollered at me. Mother Hauser might've had a Kraut moniker, but she didn't raise any fools.

I put my hands right up and said, "I'm Jim Hauser, owner of this here saloon! I apologize if I've given offense, sir!"

My fear and clear lack of any kind of comprehension of the circumstances calmed him a bit, and he put away his shooting iron. "Sorry. You had no way of knowing."

I slowly put my hands down, but not before wiping my brow. Of which there seemed to be more of every year. "That's fine, just let's keep the guns out of this. What do you say?" He didn't know it, but I had me a sawed off shotgun tucked under the bar for just such instances. I didn't grab at it, though. He was awfully quick on the draw, as I had had recent occasion to notice.

"I say sold, as long as you pour me another. And you can call me Heck." His hands were still a mite shaky, so I poured him another.

"Heck it is. That's an interesting handle, short for something?" I was tempted to pour myself something to calm the nerves, but I tried to keep away from the stuff while I was tending.

"Hector. Hector Tulane. Nice to meet you, Jim." Now, it's not every afternoon a bartender gets a pistol pointed at him, not even out here in the rough country. I was rarin' to know what Heck's story was, and besides, it was bound to be more interesting than that damn ledger.

I poured him another drink. "Same, Heck. If you don't take it as impudent, might I ask what it was I had no way of knowing?"

He shot the whiskey back clean, his hand steadying a bit. Alcohol has that effect, I'd read in a recent medical article from back East. Tobacco was considered less habit forming and better for a body, of course. "I do not take it that way, Jim. I figure you got a right to know why I done what I done, at least." he said. I figured it that way too, but I kept that to myself. He sounded like he was warming up to spin a yarn, and I didn't want to throw him.

He started where I suppose I ought to've, back close to the beginning. "I worked for the railroad back just after the war. They were rarin' to make a big push west and beat out those Pacific rail boys. You know about those boys?"

I nodded mutely, mopping at the top of bar with a rag to do something with my hands.

"Hired on coolies and the like. Pffft—" he hawked one neatly into the spittoon. I always could appreciate a man that used the facilities. "Don't matter none now. So I worked for the railroad, making sure we could build where we needed to. That means along the way we bought up parcels of land from homesteaders, pioneers and the like. Some of them folks weren't overly anxious to be rid of the land they'd fought off the red men and the bears and every other damn thing to get in the first place. My job was to convince those folks needed convincing to sell." He rolled his glass between his hands, a little smile playing around the corners of his mouth.

I had a pretty good idea of what kind of convincing he'd got up to. Old man Boehmer had been convinced into one of those shallow graves up on Boot Hill when he'd refused to sell to the rail men. Looked like Heck had enjoyed his work, anyway. He set his glass down with a raised eyebrow.

I cleared my throat. "I'll pour you another, Heck, but I wouldn't want the water getting too much deeper than this without seeing the color of your money. Sorry to say it, but there it is."

Heck fished in a pocket and brought out a couple of fine gold coins. Convincing musta paid well enough. "There you are, Jim. Just keep pouring until that's all drunk up."

I made the coins disappear.

And I kept pouring.

He kept talking. "I was in some damn part of Kentucky, about a month ahead of the cut crew, when I come upon this lovely little stead just off a crick. It was set back some up in what they call a holler in Kentucky. The road was going to have to come right through there, so I went to procure the easement from the steaders."

He drank, I poured.

"Right off I knew it was going to be one of those that took some extra convincing. The mister of the house met me right at the door, a rifle in his hands. Looked like a good piece, too, probably brought it home with him after the war. Well, he wasn't receiving visitors. Let me know it by putting shot just a few feet over my head with that damn rifle. Seems he'd heard some things about the railroad's previous dealings with local landowners and thought they were all true." He checked the front door, spooked. Like he'd heard something I hadn't.

"It's funny what we believe is true, Jim, and what we don't believe. I went back that night and set fire to his hog sty, burned up all his swine on the hoof and his straw pile. Now you know how I convinced folks."

I already had a pretty good idea before he admitted it, and I had a notion he'd done worse'n burning up a buncha pigs.

"I came back next morning, all sweetness and light, seeing if maybe he'd reconsidered his position. Before I even got up the holler, he winged me in the arm. Sumbitch musta been some shot in the army, whichever one he was in." Heck patted his arm, wincing a bit. Muscle wound like that would act up during the cold. Men at a saloon have all kinds of reasons to come in for a nip. "So I beat a hasty retreat. We weren't through, though. Not by a long chalk. I snuck back up into that holler that very same night. He'd put his boy on watch, and the kid was fast asleep. I took the old scattergun he had and threw it in the river. I wasn't about to get backshot by some wet behind the ears steader kid! I knocked him out and hog tied him for good measure."

Heck was looking right peaked. Just talking about what he was talking about was putting him a good piece back toward how he was when he walked in. I'd've figured him relishing the chance to talk about his work, he seemed the sort. Then he started to warm up again.

"I walked right up the trail to the little house. I could hear the steader in there, grunting away on top of his wife. Some are that way, needful of a woman after they get their blood up. I quieted down some, wanting to sneak up to the window and have the business done before he knew what hit him." Heck was smiling again.

I decided I didn't like his smile.

"It was the damnedest thing I ever saw. I been in the saddle plenty, if you take my meaning. This fella though, he was letting the wife ride him! She was ridin' away like she was bareback on a pony! Well, when I saw that, my plans changed a bit. A woman like that ain't an everyday occurrence, after all. I had my pistol and put one right through that fella's guts from outside the window. He give this funny little grunt, like he couldn't hardly believe it. His wife, she screamed like she was on fire, and jumped off him like he was too. I climbed in through the window and got a hold of her hair. Lucky thing was, there was still plenty of room on the bed, even with that steader bleeding out in it." Heck tossed back his whiskey and slid his glass over.

Story like this was thirsty work, I reckoned. I poured another.

He went on. "The steader, he was still livin' there, in the bed. That fella was one tough son of a bitch, I'll tell you. When I was done with the woman, I knocked her senseless and left her there. I wagged a finger under that man's nose and I said, 'See how this turned out? Is this better than getting paid to move out of the way of progress?' I told him. He gave me a look like I don't know what. Like he had all the demons of Hell right behind him, I guess. I left the both of them there and walked down the trail back to the kid. The shot and the screaming had woke him up and he was struggling to try and get a knife he had strapped to his waist. I'd tied him good though, he couldn't get at it."

I wasn't mopping at the top of the bar anymore. I was thinking about that sawed off plenty. That, and old man Boehmer, who'd been convinced right into his grave.

"I pulled that knife out and stuck it in the ground in front of the kid's face. He had that same look his Daddy'd had. 'Once I'm gone away, you cut yourself free and move you and your Momma the Hell out of here. You hear me, boy?' He didn't indicate, so I gave him a boot in the guts. When I asked again if he'd heard, he allowed that he had. I walked out of that holler and never looked back. The rail came through a month later and the place was burnt out and the people were gone. I heard there were two graves alongside the cinders and so forth, which I thought was passing odd." Heck was swaying a bit on his stool, but I couldn't tell if it shoulda been put down to his drinking or his recollecting.

I thought it was passing odd myself. Sounds of his story, the steader fella was done for, but Heck had left the wife and boy alive.

"I left that boy and his momma breathing. I went back there later, and the crosses there said 'Ma' and 'Pa.' As it turned out, that got along with what I'd found out." Heck stopped and jumped up to his feet, eyes big as pie plates. He was looking all around, his back to the wall.

I half ducked behind the bar and whispered over, "What is it Heck?"

He turned towards me and hissed back, "Sssssh! Cain't you hear that?"

I couldn't hear nothing but some big green horseflies buzzing around. "No, Heck. What d'you hear?"

"Pigs." he breathed. "Those goddamned pigs."

It took some settling, but he righted his stool and took up his glass and his yarn again. Whatever he'd heard, it had him taking less pleasure out of his tale-telling, anyway.

"Six months later, or thereabouts, I was getting some Missouri folks to sell to the railroad. It was later in the day, and I was set up in a fancy saloon and looking to get some fancy company, if you take my meaning. The big batwing doors on the place got kicked in like whoever was doin' the kickin' meant it. Standing there, all lean and hard was the kid I'd left with his Ma and dead Pa back in that holler in Kentucky. He had a gun on his hip and that look in his eye I'd seen before." Heck rubbed the grip on his pistol thoughtfully.

Since Heck was sitting here, and the kid wasn't, I guessed I knew how that fight turned out. He went and told me anyway.

"He called me out. He was walking out to the street, all ready to get it done. I shot him in the back on my way out the door and just kept on walking." Heck looked into his glass, which he was surprised to see was full. Old Heck wasn't one for letting a whiskey collect dust. He drank it down and went on. "The railroad, they like a man with a certain reputation. The kind of name that people fear and respect, both in equal parts. I 'spose a man who backshoots a revenge seeker ain't got that kind of name. They cut me loose. A month after that was the first time I heard..." Heck's throat worked convulsively, even though he wasn't drinking nothing.

"Was it the pigs, Heck?" I asked him. He looked at me with sad eyes and just nodded.

"Yeah. They caught up to me in Brisbane, then in Tuscaloosa. Each time I heard them first and then—then I saw something that wasn't possible." Heck stared at the front door again. I could hear dull thuds through the wall, which meant Cookie was choppin' up the dinner meal. I had to buy new cleavers every third month, the use they got put to back there.

"What, Heck? What did you see?" I asked him, thinking he was gonna tell about pigs. He didn't.

"That boy. He come back for me. Whatever shalla damn hole them Missouri fools put him in wasn't near enough to hold him. I've shot that boy fifty times and he just keeps coming for me. He herds his swine ahead to sniff me out, then he comes for me. Never says nothing, just keeps coming. He just keeps coming back." Heck's hand shook something fierce when he went for the glass again, and most of his liquor spilled on the bar.

I wiped it up lickety-split and poured him another, we weren't even into the second coin yet, after all.

"I ain't told anyone this whole story, Jim. Seemed like something like this happens to a fella, it's his business to deal with it. Ain't none other can carry that load, I figure. But I'm tired, Jim. Tired of running, tired of fighting. Here's where it ends. Right here." Heck tapped the bar with one finger to show me he meant my joint. I didn't cotton much to that idea. Before I could voice my concerns as a business owner, he said it again.

"Here's where it ends."

Only Heck hadn't said nothing. Whoever said them words had a voice as scratchy and dry as old straw. Whoever said those words was standing just outside the door.

Heck's neck stiffened up and he straightened up his shoulders. "Here's where it ends, kid." He walked out through the doors, and there for a moment I could hear two sets of spurs, moving apart.

Everything went quiet.

The shots erupted, and Heck gave out a scream like a stuck hog. He gasped a few times, then I figured he died out there in the street.

I could hear one set of spurs. The sound was getting closer and closer to the door of my saloon, and then a shadowy figure was standing there, outside them swinging doors. Shadowy, in full daylight. The kid pushed through and walked up to my bar. He was dried out and had bullet holes all through him, like he'd been shot to tatters. He climbed up on one of my bar stools and a shower of dust came offa his shoulders.

He worked what passed for his throat once, twice and then said in that scratchy old voice, "Whiskey."

I poured. The drinks were on Heck, I figured.

THE AIRWAY

It was Billy the Bone's bachelor party and the boys were out to have a good time. They rented a limousine to carry them around; but not just any limousine. This was one of the giant Hummer limos stocked with a full bar and enough interior room to play squash against the rear window. They were hard at it all night, and it was closing in on five in the morning. The full bar was considerably less than full and the men were running on full tanks.

"What do you want to do, Billy?" Charles asked, eager to keep the party going.

Jim spoke up, ever the voice of reason. "We've been thrown out of all the decent clubs downtown and it's already five, guys."

He was booed down and Johnny put in, "Let Billy answer! How many times is the Bone gonna get married? He should do what he wants!" Johnny had been quiet for an hour or so. His stomach was doing flip-flops like he'd been riding a roller coaster instead of a booze bottle.

Billy was sitting on the rearmost seat of the mammoth vehicle, a bottle of vodka hanging loose from one hand and a can of sugary energy drink in the other to chase the taste. "I think Dan should decide." he said.

Out of all the five men, Dan had drunk the least and smoked the most. From behind his barely open eyes he said, "Let's ride some of those motorized stairs, man." There was a moment of quiet, and they all realized that music was still playing in the car. Loud music. Then uproarious laughter broke the mood open.

"Motorized stairs. Dan! You evil genius! Where do we go to ride them?" Billy was laughing so hard he was in danger of snorting his vodka out through his nose.

"The Airway has the best ones. Some go for like, hours." Dan was fumbling for a pocket on his hooded sweatshirt, looking for another smoke.

Johnny pounded on the window between the cab and the passenger compartment, forgetting that there was an intercom. "Day-day!" They started calling their driver Day-day after the third club; his name was David Davidson. "Day-day! We gotta go to the Airway! We're gonna ride some goddamn escalators!"

The Airway was a large building in the modern style, all muted brick and steel and glass. It was still partly under construction; the parking sections were all operational but the management company's office was still being finished. Most importantly, the escalators were all online. At Billy's request, Day-day parked on the top of the ramp, the roof level. The five men piled out of the limousine, Day-day's face showing not a hint of emotion or judgment. If his clients wanted to get loaded and ride escalators, that was their business. His was to get them where they wanted to go.

"Day-day, is there any soda water in this thing?" Johnny was feeling worse than ever. His face was usually stretched in a comfortable smile, but his churning guts had him frowning hard.

"Certainly sir. Wait a moment while I get it for you." Day-

day disappeared into the cavernous innards of the limo. They stood waiting outside. Inside the car, seated, the men were mostly the same height. Standing in the wolf-light of dawn on their own unsteady feet, their differences became more clear.

Billy the Bone, the groom-to-be, was stocky, brown-haired and freckled. He wore a button down shirt, half tucked into his pants, half out; a salmon pink tie, loosened down to the third button on his shirt. Black slacks, liberally splashed with various alcoholic beverages throughout the night completed his ensemble.

His future brother-in-law, Charles had accompanied the group of old friends, but had fit in rather well. Charles had worn his favorite T-shirt, a skin-tight midnight black number with four words in elegant pink cursive on the front: "*Some Dudes Marry Dudes.*" He was right up front with his sexuality at the beginning, forgoing any weirdness with the other men. He had a solid frame and stood just a few inches shorter than Jim and Dan.

Dan wore his omnipresent green hooded sweatshirt with a large seven-pointed leaf in faded black on his chest. His black hair hung in unwashed strands around his face, just brushing his shoulders. He stared out from behind a goatee and thick glasses, the nominal reason for his medicinal use of his preferred drug. Blue jeans and ratty old sneakers completed his look. He stood as tall as Jim, who always looked the tallest since Dan usually slouched.

Jim had come correct, wearing a simple white cotton button down under a black sport coat, paired with inexpensive black chinos and shiny black shoes. Looking at him, anyone could see he had his blond hair trimmed at least weekly to keep the style optimal.

Johnny was the last of the men to get out of the car, asking for some soda water. He wore blue jeans and white T-shirt, over which he threw a comfortable tan blazer with leather patches on the elbows. He was by far the shortest of the group, and kept his hair somewhere between Jim's business style and Dan's complete lack of one. Day-day presented him with the bottle of water.

"Baby have his bottle?" Jim asked, typically poking fun. "Can we ride some escalators?" he said, to soften the blow and get a laugh.

"To the robot stairways, men!" Johnny shouted, pointing the way with his bottle.

The group ambled to the structure housing the entrance into the Airway proper and filed through it, queuing up at the top end of one of the escalators. They rode it down to the next floor, cheering all the while, except for Dan, who had a look of deepest serenity on his face. The chrome and glass building had five floors for parking and ten escalators in all, one up and one down for each floor. On the fourth floor, Charles spotted an automated photo booth.

"You guys, you guys, we have to hit that on our way out! That shit would be hilarious!" he said. His voice echoed around the mostly open space of the Airway, which prompted the rest of the men to shout things as well. The ride to the bottom was filled with laughter, grab-ass and fancy escalator riding tricks. On the first set, Jim stood on the hand rails with his arms crossed like the Colossus of Rhodes, the pressure of his weight slowed the descent of the rails and the other men passed beneath him, miming vicious uppercuts to his groin. Continuing down, Billy jumped between the two downward sets, sliding on Johnny's jacket like kid on a sled after the first snow of winter.

When they got to the bottom floor, they realized they'd timed their escalator excursion poorly, as the business trade started to flood the lobby. There were men in suits, ladies striding with purpose in clouds of perfume and everywhere there were cell phones and expensive coffee in cheap cups.

"We, uh, we better get back to Day-day." Dan said, leaning

back against one of the big chrome-encased pillars framing the large windows that made up the outer wall of the Airway's lobby.

Charles nodded in agreement. "Yeah, let's get back up to that photo booth and then get the Hell out of here. Too much business casual happening here."

"Do we take the elevator back up?" Jim put in.

"Heresy!"

"How dare you, sir?!"

"Never!"

"Elevators are for the infirm, women and the elderly!"

Jim held up his hands in surrender, laughing. "All right! All right. To our automated metal transportation!"

The ride back up was quieter, as the men shared the escalators with some third shift workers coming off the job and trudging homeward. On the third floor, Johnny had to use the bathroom.

"Hey, I'm stopping off here for a piss. Meet you guys at the booth?" he asked.

He took a ration of ribbing from his friends as he peeled off the group and headed for the the little blue sign with 'MEN'S' on it in block white letters. "More'n two shakes is playing with it, Johnny!" and "Be sure not to drop your magnifying glass in urinal this time!"

"Yeah, yeah," Johnny said under his breath, smiling, "assholes." He was already reaching for the button on his jeans when he looked up and realized he wasn't seeing the gleaming white surfaces of a modern industrial bathroom. He had somehow missed the fact the he was in one of the areas that was under construction. Pallets of construction materials wrapped in clear plastic were set seemingly at random throughout the empty area. He still needed badly to urinate.

From behind him, he heard someone yell at him. "Hey! Hey you! You can't be in here!"

"Shit." Johnny muttered, looking for a way out in front and casting glances behind.

A man in a hard hat and tool belt raised a hand over his head, waving at Johnny. "Who are you? You're not supposed to be here!"

Johnny looked all around, grabbing a glimpse of the elevator through the mostly frame-only walls. It appeared to be stuck, and the people inside were banging on the glass. A radio on Hard hat's belt squawked at him, and he grabbed at it, casting a baleful glare at Johnny. Whatever was being said on the radio made Hard hat stop his glaring and start moving back, toward the elevator. Johnny sighed in relief, and made to follow the man out of the construction zone and for God's sake find a place to piss, when three men in black suits stepped out from behind a pallet piled high with drywall.

"Who are you?" the first asked.

"You're not supposed to be in here." the second said. The other two had black, slicked down hair, but this one possessed a shock of wiry, flaming red hair. 'Danny Bonaduce red,' Jim would have said.

"You can't be in here!" the third said, indignant.

The red head put his hands up in a placating gesture. "Look, I'm the chase guy. Here," he said, reaching into his black jacket, "take this." He threw a pistol at Johnny, a snub-nosed . 38 five shot that thudded to the floor neatly at Johnny's feet, spinning slowly. Not knowing what else to do, and feeling strange as well as a little high, Johnny picked it up. He wondered briefly what the Hell Dan had put in the reefer. The three suits reached into their jackets all at once, a motion Johnny's brain, trained by a million viewings of police television programs, interpreted as going for a gun. Before he knew what was happening, he was pulling the trigger on the gun the red headed 'chase guy' had thrown to him. The firearm bucked and the explosive sounds of rounds firing was momentarily deafening.

The three men in their identical suits frowned at Johnny. None had been so much as scratched.

Johnny ran, throwing the gun away. As he passed a pallet of plywood he saw a temporary door, the kind construction workers put up to block off a room before the proper doors are installed to give themselves an enclosed lunch area, and it was ajar. Light that shifted colors from red to orange to blue to white could be seen through the crack the door was open. "Must have left a TV on in there," Johnny said incoherently, his every other thought being redirected to his screaming bladder. He pushed through the door and turned around to close it firmly. When he faced the room, nothing there made sense.

Inside the room, the most bizarre party Johnny had ever seen was taking place. Instead of some cobbled-together break room with a gas-fired camp heater and a few overturned five gallon buckets to use as chairs, there appeared to be a fully furnished video cassette rental operation. Neatly organized shelves around the walls held boxes for people to look at and little tags hung beneath to bring to the counter to rent the movies. The counter itself stood in one corner, with a curtained doorway leading into the video tape storage area. A row of free standing merchandise racks ran down the center of the room, likewise covered in the latest releases on VHS. Johnny hadn't seen a VHS tape in years.

The room was not empty, and its occupants were not shopping for video rentals. Everything was cast in a strange, pinkish light, making it hard to tell what they were wearing, but it was obvious what they were doing. Glasses clinked together over toasts and the chattering of party goers made the music that was playing unintelligible. A woman wearing an old style bunny outfit and carrying a tray of tobacco products approached him.

"Cigarette sir?" she asked.

He nodded mutely, accepting the heater and jamming it in his mouth. Johnny leaned forward to touch the end to the flame of the match the cigarette girl had lit, and he thought he saw Hulk Hogan, the professional wrestler, in the back of the room, near the drama section of the store. He got a good draw going, then realized he had lit the filter end of his heater. He held it away from his mouth, disgusted with his stupidity. Why was he even smoking? He'd quit years ago. Many of the other people in the strange pinkish light had butts in their hands, in their mouths. Johnny observed that the tobacco burned down extraordinarily fast, as if he were watching the cigarettes, and the cigarettes only, in some kind of time lapse.

Back in the corner by the Hulkster, the crowd started to jostle and shift. The three men in black suits suddenly shoved their way through the throng.

"Hey! Who are you!" one of them challenged him. The red head was in the lead, and when he got close enough, Johnny flicked his still-burning cigarette in the suit's face. Then he ran for the door. Behind him, as he spared one last look, he saw the three men had stopped chasing him, and had sad looks on their faces as they watched him go.

Outside the door, Johnny found himself back in the general area of the Airway. He felt different, somehow. *Day-day.* he thought, *that bastard Day-day put something in the water that disagreed with what ever the Hell Dan gave me to smoke.* He stopped running and took momentary stock of the situation. He had to get to the roof, and the limousine. Dan. Dan would know how to handle someone having a bad trip. He had to call Dan.

Johnny dipped into his jacket pocket to grab his cell phone, but the pocket wasn't where he'd left it. His hand hit the side of his black jacket and slid off. He looked down wonderingly. He was wearing an unrelieved black suit. Unrelieved, that was, except for his gold tie. It was one of his work suits, and not even his favorite one. Johnny shook his head. He had to get to the roof. He looked around, searching for the quickest way up.

The people walking by him weren't staring, exactly. They all had that look in the eye that signified 'Yes, we know each other. Hello.' An old Asian couple walked by, the woman waved and the man said, "A bold display! Like Chu-san!"

Johnny shook his head and made for the elevators. *Fucking escalators*, he thought. The doors to the elevator stood blessedly open, as if they were waiting just for him. He practically ran in, jamming the 5 button and then savaging the —>| |<— button. A blonde wearing glasses, a ponytail, volleyball shorts and a purple backpack approached the doors as they were sliding closed. Johnny nearly stuck his hand out reflexively, but checked himself.

"Get the next one, volleyblonde," he began to mutter to his reflection. Before he got to 'next' a horrible screeching interrupted him. He felt the stomach churning vertigo he'd been experiencing since earlier, only multiplied exponentially, and then the sounds of rending metal and shattering glass stopped all conscious thought.

He awoke feeling a flying sensation, interrupted by the sound he imagined a wad of hamburger might make if shot out of a cannon at a brick wall. He opened his eyes, and there was a strange pink color to everything he saw. Suddenly, a figure towered over him. The volleyblonde.

"Who are you?" She asked nonsensically, in shock from seeing his torn and broken body.

I just saved your life, he thought. *Then, No, how long have I been laying here? Why can't I get up? No. No! Nononononononono* He lay dying, trying to force his mind back into the memory he had of Billy's bachelor party, three years previous.

GRIST

He didn't know if it was the water heater or softener or the furnace, but some piece of machinery in that basement put out a constant hum that set his teeth on edge. The sheer malignancy of it could be felt through the soles of his feet even on the top floor of the house. It wasn't until after his sister-in-law died that he started to notice it in other places.

Brenda served in Iraq for four years before joining what she called the '1st Civilian brigade, all POG division.' Ty often remembered her that way, throwing some cryptic acronym at him. He thought of all her military jargon as Brenda-isms. It was only at her funeral that he realized there was an entire culture of people who spoke her same language. Had he heard the hum there? It was hard to think about a time when he hadn't been able to pick it out of the ambient noise everywhere he went. An undertone that felt like grinding, somewhere in his back teeth.

After what happened in the basement with Brenda, neither he nor his wife Carol wanted to go down there again, finished or not. Ty wanted the finished basement as much as Carol wanted the two car garage while they were house hunting. That was why Brenda had been visiting that week to begin with, to see the new house.

Looking at it from the driveway, she'd said "Within spitting distance of New York City, if you had a map of New York and felt like spitting on it." Brenda's home base was Chicago, so she thought the Iowa suburban locale Ty and Carol had chosen to start a family was a little dull. It suited Carol and he just fine, however. They'd lived in a tiny apartment for two years scrimping and saving the down payment, dreaming all the while about getting out of there and into a home where they didn't share a wall with a neighbor. All that was before what happened in the basement.

Ty had mapped out the movements of all the pieces with metronomic precision: He picked up Brenda from the airport thirty minutes early.

"Since when is a flight early?" she asked him, lugging her suitcase. "You civ sector types really have to get on the hurry up and wait program." They both laughed.

The ride home took an hour. Ty parked the car in the driveway, and Carol met them out front. Brenda looked at the house and talked about the relative distance to a big city. Carol showed Brenda around the house, until his sister-in-law declared, "Did the carpet in this basement arrive standard issue fatigue green, or did you install it just so I'd leave your man-cave alone? I need a nap and a shower. Can do, Ty?" He smiled, she always treated him like a grunt. Carol decided they needed a box of wine, and asked Ty to drive her to the store.

They left Brenda there alone.

She went straight to the basement bathroom, the shower Ty and Carol had readied for guests, without her loofas and scented soaps or Ty's harshly astringent idea of soap. The noise of the quick shower masked the sounds of the front door being opened and heavy steps on the stairs.

At the first stoplight intersection en route, the system was broken down. The lights in all four directions blinked red to indicate that four-way stop rules should be used instead. A young person unfamiliar with the rules went out of turn, crunching into the vehicle whose driver had the the right of way. Ty and Carol leaned out of their windows, trying to get a look past the massive white Escalade sitting in front of them.

His wife asked him, "Think the designers at Cadillac could make them any bigger?"

"How do you think they keep selling them each year? Add an inch." They smiled at each other, enjoying their inside marriage talk.

Brenda toweled off and got dressed, all without knowing there was someone else in the house. When a hand clamped down over her mouth, her training and instincts took over as she stomped down on where her attacker's instep should be and she went into fluid motion that would have broken the wrist attached to the hand over her mouth. Only the attacker hadn't responded to his instep being crushed. The police reports released after the trial said that the man had four bones in his foot broken, but he still kept his grip, one arm around Brenda's throat and a hand over her mouth.

Sitting idling with the air conditioning on while the intersection was cleared of the accident dropped the car's fuel reserve below 50%. Ty pulled into a gas station.

"Hon? What's up?" Carol asked.

"Gotta get gas." he answered, terse. The fun, snarky comments had mostly run out. There was a metallic taste in the back of his throat, from what he assumed was sucking Escalade exhaust through the car's ventilation. Carol hated it that he insisted on filling up at half a tank. He had shown her on paper how it got them better mileage, but it still annoyed her. At the counter, the first card he presented was declined. They fought about it the rest of the way to liquor store.

Brenda did damage, even though her ability to do so was curtailed by the loss of most of the fingers on her right hand. After the man came back with the hammer and nails, the coroner's report was inconclusive as to how long she survived.

Ty stood next to Carol as the checkout girl at the liquor store ran the box of wine, complete with duck on the front, over the staring red electric eye that calculated the price. His phone buzzed in his pocket as he pulled out his wallet, sending his other hand diving for it. A quick look at the caller ID that read 'Rollie Cell' before Ty swiped to answer and pinched the phone between his shoulder and ear.

"Rollie, buddy. What's up?" Ty answered genially.

"Ty, I need a favor pal." Rollie's voice came over the line, sounding oddly tinny and little distorted. *Bad service in here* Ty remembered thinking *or he's got me on speaker.* "The wife picked out a new couch," Rollie went on, his voice picking up a buzzing undertone that Ty found disquietingly familiar though he didn't know why at the time, "and I need help moving the old one out to the garage."

Ty smiled emptily at the counter girl, juggling the wallet and trying to hand the card to the cashier, who looked bored and pointed to the credit card reader bolted to a plate in front of him. Rollie doggedly continued, as Ty had known he would. "I'm offering beer and time away from the domestic unit. What say?" That was Rollie all over, trying save the fee the dump would charge him for getting rid of his couch. He'd put it in the garage, sit on it once a year and feel like he was putting one over on somebody.

Ty glanced over at Carol, saw her pointedly not paying attention to his conversation, which of course meant she was listening to every word. "No can do, Rollie. Got the sister-in-law in town, and we got plans." Ty surprised himself with an actual grin as he used a Brenda-ism and with the feeling of anticipation he felt. He really had missed his wife's sister, and he hadn't realized until just that moment.

They arrived home to flashing red lights. The noises coming from the house had been loud enough to alert even neighbors that they didn't share walls with. Ty had read the police reports obsessively to determine where each event fell on the time line, but what he recalled most vividly was the man the officers led out of his house. Spattered in gore and limping badly, his voice was monotone as he kept repeating the same thing.

"I never meant to kill her. It was an error. I never meant to kill her. It wa—" until the door slammed as he was shoved into a waiting squad car. Ty locked eyes with the man for a moment, and something was missing. It only lasted a moment; but later, in his private moments, Ty would see those eyes again. The pupils had eaten up all the color of the iris, leaving only the whites, with a big black circle in each one. It lasted only a moment, and then the man shook his head unsteadily and looked all around. A moment later he began thrashing, but just as quickly stopped when he seemed to notice the bloodstains and worse on his clothes.

They knew they had to move out of the house, but they didn't have the financial wherewithal. Neither one of them wanted to go in the basement. Ty wasn't quite hearing that insistent, metallic grinding anywhere but in the basement, not yet. Then what seemed like perfect kismet dropped on them during a church service. A new pastor was moving to town to take over for the retiring pastor at their church, but the retiring man wouldn't be moved out of the pastorage for another six months. Rather than have the congregation get up a collection for a rental, the idea was put forward that a member of the flock board the new preacher and his family. Carol wasn't wild about it, but Ty immediately seized on the idea. How better to change his and his wife's perception of the basement than to make new memories of it? The new man, Pastor Hayes, could plainly see that the couple needed counseling and help in dealing with their loss. He assented to moving his wife and two children into the basement.

Things were strange, at first. The conversations between Carol, Ty and Pastor Hayes usually ran in the same directions. They talked about death and God's plan for each person; how Jesus died on the cross for all of humanity's sins, stabbed to death by a bored legionary and all the passion the son of God had had to go through. Gradually, things became less strange. The Hayes kids tromping on the stairs, Mrs. Hayes asking to bring a table into the basement so she could keep home schooling the kids without disturbing Carol and Ty, Pastor Hayes' adorable habit of hanging the laundry out to dry whenever possible to minimize the electric bill, all of these things combined to take the sharp, jagged edges off the memory of Brenda's death. It became something that had happened in the past instead of something they had to get up and look in the face every morning. Even though things became less strange, there were still odd moments. Ty would recall later that Pastor Hayes often asked him about maintenance on household equipment like water pumps and air conditioners. It wasn't until Carol called him at work to tell him she was pregnant that he put those questions together with the sound that seemed to be seeping into other aspects of his life.

As Carol was saying "Honey, I have great news that can't wait...", he was looking under his desk to check his computer. Something under there had been making an unpleasant mechanical noise for weeks. That was when he knew he'd heard the noise before. It matched the strange feedback he was getting on the line with Carol. "I'm pregnant, Ty!" He sat up fast, forgetting the desk, bonking his head on it. He cursed, rubbing the back of his head. "What." his wife replied.

"I said, are you sure? This is great," even he himself sounded strange to his ear, so he tried again. "This is incredible! We're going to be parents? We're going to be parents! I'm coming home." Before she could even reply, he threw the receiver of his phone in the direction of the base unit and headed for the door. His brief sense memory connection about the clicking, grinding sound was forgotten, but he would have cause to make it again, and soon.

Carol must have driven the car last, because the fuel gauge rested directly over the large, red 'E' on the left hand side. After a brief flash of annoyance that was immediately smothered by the warm glow he was still feeling over the great news he'd just received, he pulled into a filling station. At the counter, the first card he handed over was declined. Something in the back of his mind turned over. He dismissed the feeling and reached for the cash in the back of his wallet.

Inspiration hit as he drove past a nursery, and he pulled into the lot; mind set on a bouquet of flowers with lots of baby's breath to fill. As the cashier punched the keys on the antiquated IBM cash register, he felt his phone vibrate in his pocket. The screen read 'Rollie Cell' and that feeling came back, spurred on heavily by the unthinking static buzzing of the vibration motor in his phone. He swiped the screen gingerly to answer.

Before he knew he was going to say it, "Rollie, buddy. What's up?" came out of his mouth.

"Ty, hey, I just dropped by your desk, but you were gone." *Speaker phone*, Ty thought to himself unconvincingly, *that's what that noise is.* "I wanted to ask if you and Carol or maybe Pastor Hayes had any interest in my old grill." Rollie's voice was flat, rote, as if he were reading from cue a card that didn't have punctuation.

"Sir? The total?" The cashier tapped the green dot matrix screen, and Ty pinched the phone between his shoulder and ear, thumbing through his wallet. He took out the card he'd used at the gas station and tried handing to the girl. She motioned at a reader bolted to a plate in front of him. That was when he looked at the girl behind the counter, and really saw her for the first time. He was certain it was the same person that had been behind the counter at the liquor store the day that Brenda died. He hung up on Rollie and half walked, half ran to his car.

The stoplight was broken, just like he knew it would be. He left the car sitting behind a gigantic SUV he barely looked at as he ran flat-out for home, leaving the cyclopean, blinking red lights of the intersection and the accident there behind.

He came through the front door of the house soaked in sweat. The building was quiet, but he could hear the blood pounding in his ears. That, and something else. Something he had tried to block out since Brenda had died so badly. He cast one look at the door to the basement, which the Hayes kept closed to give he and Carol privacy, before taking the stairway up and into the main living area. Carol was sitting on the couch, a book in one hand. She looked up at him.

"Ty? I didn't hear the car pull up. Why are you sweating?" He answered by gathering her up in his arms and crushing her with a hug.

"Nothing, it's nothing. I just had to see you," he told her, letting her go. "There was an accident."

"Oh my God, are you okay?" she asked, looking him all over, fluttering hands on his arms.

"Yeah, just scared myself silly over nothing. I need a minute to sort myself out." He went to the kitchen, dropping an ice cube in a tumbler and splashing scotch on top of it. His hands shook as the adrenaline of his mad run wore off. That thing in the back of his mind had been wrong. That twisty feeling of vertigo telling him he'd been here, he'd done all this before was all for nothing. He stepped out through the patio door and stood on the deck, draining half his glass in a convulsive gulp. The warmth of the alcohol was just starting to bloom in his still queasy gut when he heard an unmistakable click to his left.

A male voice said, "This is an error. There was a malf—"

Ty turned and tossed his drink, glass and all into the man's face. The man instinctively raised his hands to ward off the attack, taking the gun off Ty. While the gun was pointed up, Ty rushed him, taking in the details of his clothes in the elongated seconds between jumping at and hitting. The man wore a denim jacket, heavily worn and lightly washed. Dirt was caked into the creases of the garment and into the creases on the man's face. Though the man's eyes were slitted against the liquid dripping into them, Ty could see with horror that the pupils were as big around as the mouth of the gun barrel that was coming back level with his chest.

They impacted. Ty's shoulder knocked the man's gun hand away, and a single shot crashed off harmlessly into the garage door. They hit the wood planks of the patio and Ty went into a frenzy of punching, kicking, biting and slamming the man down over and over again. It took seconds for Ty to discern that the man was flopping boneless under the battering. The gun had fallen away from the man's hand after that first shot.

Ty straddled him, ready to begin pummeling again at the first sign of aggression. The man was blinking, his eyes a very normal brown as he looked owlishly around.

"Wait," he said, confused, "it's not breakfast time."

The police were taking down the final version of Ty's statement. The guy was in the back of a squad car, safely cuffed. "So then I waited for you guys to arrive after my wife called 9-1-1."

The police officer typed a few sentences into his tablet. "I see, sir. Just one last question: is there anyone who would want to hurt you or your family, anyone who might have sent this man?"

Ty shook his head. "No, there isn't anyone. The only person I know of who wanted to hurt us is sitting in prison for killing my wife's sister."

The officer raised an eyebrow but didn't pursue the line of questioning. He had clearly been briefed on the events of a year ago. "Alright then, sir. Are there any questions you have for me?"

Ty almost immediately answered in the negative, just wanting the interview to be over so he could talk to Carol and hold her tight. Instead he asked, "Has anyone talked to Pastor Hayes? He might have a better view of who in the community might want to hurt anyone."

The officer tapped an entry into his device. "Ah, no. It appears no one has questioned your renter."

Ty ignored the error, it was a common one. "Could you get him out here, please? I'm sure he must be worried sick." Ty hugged the thin blanket the EMTs had given him a bit more tightly around his shoulders as the officer nodded and waved over another couple of uniforms while talking into his radio. Ty looked for his wife and daughter near the ambulance, but got distracted by the look of consternation on the officer's face as something about the pastor was discussed.

A plainclothes female police broke away from the conversation to address Ty. "Sir, you're the owner here?"

He nodded.

"Do we have permission to enter your renter's unit?" she asked.

"Uh, they're more like boarders. What's going on here?" Ty asked, not sure what he meant.

"We'd like your permission before entering the domicile, sir.

May we have it?" She doggedly ignored his question. He nodded again, not sure what else to do. Several officers lined up on either side of the door into the basement, weapons drawn and grim looks on their faces. They nodded to each other and the plainclothes police took the door, weapon in one hand and flashlight on the other. It was completely dark in the basement, the door looking like a giant square of black that was methodically eating up the police officers and their lights as they moved tactically into it. Ty followed them, expecting to be directed away by one of the officers at any second, but they all seemed to ignore him.

The darkness in the basement was complete. The flashlights of the police seemed like bad jokes, illuminating only a tiny circle of the endless abyss the basement of his family's home had turned into. Something in the dark was crunching. A wet slurping crunch, crunch, crunch, crunch. Then it stopped.

Then it began again. Ty watched as the flashlights of the officers slowly converged on the sound. Pastor Hayes was sitting at his family's dining room table, eating a bowl of cold cereal. The box sat just in front of him, a jaunty cartoon sea captain waving from the side of it. The milk jug, 2% Ty knew by the bright blue cap, was on the pastor's right. The lights centered on the preacher. He sat nearly unmoving, spooning up the breakfast food with abbreviated, mechanical movements. He did not look around as the lights hit him, he simply sat and ate.

Ty knew the basement like only a person who lives in a house can know a basement. He reached for a light switch and flicked it on before he could think to stop himself.

The rest of the family, wife and two kids, sat at the table with Pastor Hayes, their faces buried in bowls of soggy cereal. Great red circles were spread out beneath each of them. Each of their throats was slashed. Blood trails led to each chair, showing that they were carried in after the fact and left to bleed their last at the table.

Pastor Hayes stopped chewing when the light came on. His mouth opened, a lump of half-masticated food dropping back into the bowl he was hunched over. He looked at Ty, and the pupils of his eyes ate up all the color. The preacher's eyes were white with a black circle of pupil that stared out at Ty with all the emotion of a lawn mower.

"A death is required. There will not be a third mistake." it said.

Ty turned and ran up the stairs, looking for his wife. The insistent, unthinking, grinding sound filled his ears and a metallic, coppery taste filled his mouth.

Dead Man's Medicine

It was only after I swallowed the pills that I realized the bottle I held in my hand was dead man's medicine. He had cancer, he was old and one day, he died. There was a hole where he once was, but I hadn't really felt it. Not yet. Even though the man had been in the ground for months, the only thing I was feeling at that moment was a headache; and brother, it was a doozy. The kind of headache that starts as a pulse behind the eyes and turns into me lying in a dark room with a wet washcloth over my eyes, whimpering as quietly as possible. Lucky for me, I caught it the behind the eyes phase, and when I can do that I can generally kill it with enough acetaminophen. I checked the label on the dead man's bottle for dosage information. I should have figured that a cancer patient would probably be on a slightly higher number of milligrams than are available over the counter. Of course, it only occurred to me to check after I shotgunned three of them.

The day was an odd one. The male members of the family had met up to split up a lifetime's worth of tools, fishing gear and other potent man artifacts. I was there to pick over these items and take any that I thought I could find a use for. It didn't hit me that I was pawing over history. Not right away. Stuff like that always sneaks up on a man.

Here's a circular saw blade still in the plastic, and there's one just as new on the saw itself. What isn't apparent there are the plans for building a fence frame to keep those damn rabbits out of the garden once and for all, or putting together tomato crates.

Here's a home made worm shocker, just a length of steel with one end of an extension cord wired onto it and a wooden handle to stop the current running up your arm. You jam it in the ground, plug it in and pick up the worms as they crawl out of the dirt. What's missing here is the story of seeing one on TV or some damn place and thinking, 'Hell, I can make that.' And he did. And it works like a charm.

There's a cheap old plastic tackle box with an In-Fisherman sticker on it. Sure doesn't look like much. It just so happens to be the first plastic tackle box the man ever bought sometime back when Plano first started making them out of plastic so the bastard things would stop rusting.

Here are rusted chunks of metal that at one time served as tools to the family a generation or two ago. Objects so unfamiliar to our modern sensibilities we can only guess at what functions they may have performed for those people without whose toil, struggle, love and laughter we would not exist.

These stories didn't occur to me as I stood there, dazed with pain, and when that was gone, with powerful painkillers. None of them. Not until some passerby stopped and asked if we were having a garage sale. We weren't, as you know, but that didn't stop him putting his oar in. He turned out to be quite knowledgeable about antique fishing tackle and pocket knives. He started throwing out probable prices for this, that and the other thing.

That's when it hit me. Right then, right between the eyes, and harder than the migraine. This guy didn't have a clue what he was talking about. A man's whole life in tools and gear laid out and all he saw was dollar signs. That, though, that wasn't the realization that hit me hardest.

All that stuff, all those things, those pills I had swallowed earlier, they weren't what was left of the man who was gone.

We were. All of us there together, we were what he had left behind that mattered, not a garage full of stuff. As I looked around at the other men in my family, they didn't seem to be affected by my epiphany. Of course they weren't. They all knew it already, one way or another.

All those stories were there, and I hadn't heard but a few of them, but it didn't matter. We did. We did; to him, and to each other. It took me awhile, and I suspect longer than most, but I suppose it's a lesson we all come to; whether or not we ever take a dead man's medicine.

Afterword

When I first thought about putting this collection together, the afterword was very much on my mind. Would anyone reading this want to see behind the curtain at what made these stories get up and go? Being honest I wondered first if anyone would read this at all, and *then* what the hypothetical reader would want out of it. I decided against breaking down the collection tale by tale, and instead I'm going to let you, dedicated reader of authorial notes, in on my big secret. It's this: most of my short stories start out as dreams. I'm not sure what deeply buried machinery in my psyche does the heavy lifting, creatively speaking, but sometimes I think it generates the same hum that Ty first hears in his basement back on page 211.

I would be remiss now not to give thanks to the many individuals without whom a book is impossible, so here is a in no way ordered or exhaustive list: My Grandma Eva, who you read about in the dedication. Thanks for letting me read The Berenstein Bears and the Spooky Old Tree, Gramma. Me Ma and my Pops, you both know who you are and what you did. The Bear. Mark Johnston, Ben Wheeler-Floyd, Phil and his daughter Liz for moral support and timely editorial input. Aron Robison, Jon Fratzke and Steve Bein for the loan of some intellectual properties. Thanks also to Jon's wife Leah, who makes her home our home away from home. Thanks as well to Ben Mulholland and his wife Hannah, whose home's layout I used in one of these stories and for the valuable feedback. Matt and Neil at emendesign for the terrific work on all my covers, you guys are a treat to work with!

Here is where the tearful goodbyes and promises to see each other soon would mark the end of our time together, but I feel like you've earned a little something, sticking in here until the end. You've read all my thank yous, whether or not they meant anything to you personally. Those thanks and the fact that you read them means the world to me. In return, here's an extra story. Everyone that skipped past this bit to put up their reviews on Amazon or Goodreads or ran to Tweet about finishing the book doesn't get this one. It's just for us.

Happily Never After

Once upon a time, a common girl with an uncommon heart accompanied four heroes on a quest to lift a curse on a strange and backward kingdom ruled from a castle under a mountain. Their victory was hard fought, and cost them all dearly, but in the end, the girl was crowned Queen and ruled justly over her revitalized kingdom. One by one her heroes left the castle under the mountain to seek their fortunes elsewhere until only one was left, and him she married.

So just and so kind was her rule that a strange visitant of old times, wise in the ways of kings and queens, came to her to be her adviser. In time, the people came to call this strange creature Verouth.

In time, the people came to fear Verouth.

It was said that the beast (and so the people named this visitant, for he resembled a great featherless bird in feature and had the claws of a giant bear on his hands) could become invisible at will, and was willing to strike down any who spoke against the increasingly heavy taxes the Queen and her King enforced on the people. The people began to question the formerly peaceable rule of their Queen, and the more people questioned, the more people disappeared.

Tales were told of the castle under the mountain, tales of horror and cruelty and blood.

The more tales were told, the more tale-tellers disappeared.

"We have to do something. This is our fault, much as anyone's." The big man who spoke had a thick beard that was gray going to white. The chainmail byrnie he wore was spotted in places with rust. His thick, scarred hands rested on the table, holding a steaming tankard.

Across the table from him, a bald old man tapped a small steel hammer against a sheet of bronze thin as paper and light as a feather. "I agree with you," he said, "we should confront them, face to face, and find out what is happening."

The big man blew across the top of his drink, cooling the liquid enough to drink. He took a sip, and licked his lips. "Aye, and find the truth behind this beast, Verouth." If the small inn was quiet before, naming the form of fear silenced it completely.

The third man at the table was shrouded in a thin linen garment, and a gauzy hood obscured his features. "It is decided then. Tomorrow we go to court and treat with our Queen."

The great entrance to the cavern under the mountain that held the castle was flanked by statues, thrice and thrice again as tall as a man. One was a roaring bearded warrior carrying sword and shield, the other a thin man holding a complicated crossbow pointed downward.

"Fine stonework, this." The big man gestured toward the statuary.

The thin old man sniffed, adjusting the shoulder strap that slung a crossbow over his shoulder. "A bit gaudy for my tastes."

The wasn't much traffic going in to or out of the gateway, yet as all petitioners were welcome at the court of the Queen in the Undercastle, their passage went unchallenged by the heavily armed and armored guards that seemed to be omnipresent.

"Bloody job lot of guards," the man in linen said, "what do you suppose they are meant to guard?" He shuffled forward behind his two friends, leaning on an old, gnarled staff.

The courtyard's cold gloom was only partly warmed by the presence of six golden shafts of sunlight shining down ducts carved through the mountain. Beneath each duct, a great tree stood, small bunches of withered leaves here and there among the branches the only sign that they still lived.

"Still don't like those things." the big man muttered to the others.

"You don't?" The man in linen turned his hooded face, seeming to pass his gaze over each of the old wood titans. "I find them... Serene."

The great draw bridge spanned the moat before the castle, running deep with swift, dark water. Standing in front of the great levers that facilitated its operation on the far side were two more statues. One was a lithe man, a long-handled hammer held in both his hands, the other a man in simple traveling robes, his hood thrown back and leaning on a strange, smooth-surfaced staff.

"Doesn't seem right to me," said the big man, looking up, "he never made it this far."

The man with the crossbow tapped his friend on the arm. "Hush. It's a good likeness."

"So it is." agreed the last man, following on.

The entry hall was flanked with great stone pillars, each carved with scenes of battle featuring the figures depicted in the four statues engaged in battle against various horrific monsters, along with a fifth figure. She was beautiful, even carved in still stone. Her grace and clever mind somehow showed through in each of the tales that the pillars were meant to tell.

"Was it really like that?" asked the man in linen.

"Does it matter now?" said the old man, by way of answer.

"Aye." said the big man, answering them both.

The doors to the throne room were thrown wide, though guards stood by on each hand. The three men walked on, paying them no mind. As they entered the richly appointed royal chamber, the doors were swung shut behind them. On her throne sat the Queen of the Undercastle, and she was as beautiful as all the carvings in the entry hall, and more.

Her skin was moonlight on mahogany, her hair spun gold shot through with obsidian. The circle of metal around her brow looked as if it had always been there. Two steps below her throne on the dais was another chair, less ornate and empty. The men approached, and fell to one knee.

"My Queen," one rumbled.

"Queen Alysanne of the Undercastle," the old man agreed.

"M'lady?" asked the man in linen.

"Rise. Rise, my old friends! What brings you back here, after all this time?" she asked them, a furrow wrinkling her nearly non-existent freckles prettily.

They rose, and the old man spoke. "I think you know, your Majesty. Tales are told of your court."

The Queen laughed as she did most everything, musically and with grace. "Tales? Tales are told of snakes born with a head at either end, and calves with power of speech."

The big gray man shook his shaggy head. "Dark tales, Aly-girl. Tales such as were told about this place before we lifted the curse."

"Bloody tales," agreed the man leaning on his old staff.

"Bloody tales is all they are," said a new voice, a man's voice, "and you're all old fools if you believe otherwise." From the

Queen's left, behind the shrouded curtains that hid the royal entrance sauntered a young nobleman with boyish features in a skin-tight velvet doublet and hose. A plainer, simpler metal ring circled his brows and he draped himself over the lower chair.

"Aye," said the big man, grinding his teeth, "and who might you be to wear that crown and sit that chair, pup?"

The Queen laughed again, this time with an edge that cut. "Don't you recognize your old friend Dirk, Barlen? Is aught amiss?"

"Dirk? A blind man could see that it is not." The man in linen pushed back his filmy hood, revealing a face that was both young and old at the same time, ageless. White scars covered every visible inch of his skin, branching in every direction.

"He is who I say he is. For am I not Queen? Do I not wear the crown and sit the throne of the Undercastle?" the Queen questioned them, the teasing note in her voice not veiling a hard and accusing tone.

"You are and you do, Queen Alysanne. These facts are not in question. What you have done with our friend is; for no matter what you decree, that fop is not him." The bald old man's hand shook a bit as he pointed to the young man on the dais.

The Queen frowned in a moue of mock sadness. "Is that a touch of palsy I detect, Sebastian? A shame, a terrible shame. Your days of making clever little toys must be at end." She waved her hand at them, dismissing them. "When my Verouth told me you were coming, I was excited to see my old friends whom I honored with accolades and statues. However, I find myself growing most bored with you. You may leave."

Barlen bristled at being dismissed. "We'll not leave, Aly-girl, not until we have the truth of what's become of you. Aye, that, and the truth behind this beast Verouth."

"Yes, let us see this dread Verouth that takes dissenters and tellers of tales in the night. Surely it cannot be that you've brought back one of the visitants we strove against." Sebastian was casually swinging his crossbow off his shoulder and into his hands, a motion without thought or misfire, so often had it been performed.

"Visitant? Visitant? Visitants are from away, while my Verouth and those like him were always here to advise me. Verouth, you may take these boring people to the dungeons for the evening's entertainment." the Queen appeared to address the air, speaking her voice raised and a note of command.

A strangely familiar whistling sound was the only warning Barlen had as something slammed into his back, driving him to his knees.

"Yes! Yes! Set the beast on them!" The fop had abandoned his languid posture and was perched on the edge of his seat, smiling and laughing. The Queen frowned momentarily at him and he quieted immediately.

Pariah had been badly mauled by the hungry trees in the battle to take the Undercastle years ago before he realized that the only way to beat them was to meet their blood lust with emptiness. He had sat and absorbed their hatred, allowing it to fall into the void of a mind that knew no concept of self, or thought or intent. He put himself in that state again, blocking the first whistling, invisible blow directed at him, then a second and a third. Finally, age and infirmity betrayed him, and his guard slipped for a split second, fracturing his perfect defense. The blow turned his knee into a crimson blossom of blood and pain.

Sebastian, the toymaker, turned the last dial and flipped the last switch on his beloved master work, his most constant companion, with a whispered farewell. It, and he, exploded into a hundred tiny fragments.

A hundred doves, all wrought from the material of the weapon that had served the old man all his life and animated by the life force of the man himself flitted from perch to perch. They flew about the great chamber, their wings producing the unique whistling that was the only thing that could break the invisibility of the beast that was Verouth.

Towering over the fallen Pariah was Verouth, the beast himself. His shape and dimensions were well known to the men who had destroyed the remains of the visitants in this very hall. It stood tall and thin with broad, broad shoulders and arms ending in strange clawed hands with two long fingers above the palm and two long fingers below. Most of his body was hidden by a voluminous cloak but above his shoulders perched a birdlike head, with tiny black eyes and a pointed fleshy beak lined with teeth.

In one hand he wielded a long-handled hammer. The beast growled, and a deviant might have called it laughter.

Barlen shoved himself to his feet, gripping his shield and drawing his sword. "Here, beast. I'm your man."

Verouth turned, and the light caught two shining lines of white scar tissue stretching back up his scalp from an old wound.

The big old man slammed the cross guard of his sword against the rim of his shield. "Aye, me. And I'll have my friend's hammer back from you after, monster."

The Queen erupted in mirth, but Barlen had no time to wonder at it. The beast was on him, swinging the hammer in tight, expert arcs and supplementing his attacks with his wicked claws. Barlen started out trading one blow for two, then one for three, then one for five, and soon it was all he could do to defend himself. Wood chips flew from his shield as the hammer came in again and again until the head of the weapon finally caught on the rim, dragging the old warrior off balance. He stumbled and fell, landing badly and barely escaping impaling himself in his own sword.

Verouth stalked forward to finish Barlen.

"Dirk," said Pariah from the floor, "Dirk, listen. This form she's twisted you into was made for hearing, so hear me: You are not what you have become. What little power I have to heal, I use. I cannot heal your body, it has been warped beyond my ability. All I can heal is your mind." Pariah tapped the end of his staff on the floor of the carpeted throne room once, weakly. The light went out of his blind eyes as he lay gently down, a small smile on his lips.

Verouth howled. He dropped his hammer, and placed his malformed hands on his head as he remembered being a man and being loved and being a monster and being hated.

"Verouth, my Verouth. Come back to your Queen." Alysanne purred from her throne.

Verouth, the beast, reached down, his hand an inch from his hammer.

Barlen was on his feet before he realized he had been picked up.

"mm drrrk" the thing in front of him said, grasping Barlen's sword hand and putting the tip of the blade at its own throat. "mm drrrk" it repeated.

"Dirk," Barlen choked out.

The big man thrust forward cleanly, saving his old friend.

The Queen spoke. "Barlen. Barlen, you have no idea what it is to rule. Dirk-that-was never did either. The secrets of turning men into beasts like my Verouth were born of the first King of the Undercastle. He knew secrets you cannot fathom."

The big man walked up the steps to the throne on unsteady legs that felt like wood.

"You four never understood about the curse, not truly. It was never on the kingdom, it was on the crown. Cruel King Antilar just turned it from in to outward."

He threw his shattered shield away, steadying the wavering

blade with a two handed grip.

"It takes in all the bad thoughts, the sins, the evil that my people would do to each other. It was made in friendship with the dwarfs, but the minds of men were never meant to rule this way."

Barlen stumbled on the top step, falling to one knee.

"I thought a woman could do it, could wear the crown and rule and be and do all the things a good Queen is and does. But it doesn't matter who wears it," she said, standing and walking to him, she all grace and beauty and him a bloody mess. She rested a hand on his head in benediction "the crown is cursed."

"Then let's have it off you, Aly-girl." he said, pushing himself to his feet and raising his sword.

www.ingramcontent.com/pod-product-compliance
Lightning Source LLC
Chambersburg PA
CBHW031959240626
47153CB00003B/1043